DR MALONE, I PRESUME?

Abby Andrews was determined not to join the half of the world that loved the dark and devastating Dr Sam Malone. Sam was a hero, a medical idealist who had worked to save lives in the trouble-spots of the world. But did that give him the right to make Abby feel guilty for having settled for the good life?

Dr Malone,
I Presume?

by
Holly North

Magna Large Print Books
Long Preston, North Yorkshire,
England.

British Library Cataloguing in Publication Data.

North, Holly
 Dr Malone, I presume?

A catalogue record for this book is
available from the British Library

ISBN 0-7505-0633-4

First published in Great Britain by Mills & Boon Ltd., 1987

Published in Large Print 1994 by arrangement with Harlequin
Enterprises B.V., Switzerland.

Magna Large Print is an imprint of
Library Magna Books Ltd.
Printed and bound in Great Britain by
T.J. Press (Padstow) Ltd., Cornwall, PL28 8RW.

CHAPTER ONE

'Ouch!' James Farris gripped the arms of the sofa on which he was lying and groaned as if he was being murdered. The towel that covered his buttocks began to slip and Abby, kneeling on the floor beside him, smacked him briskly on the bottom, covered him up again, and resumed the massage.

'Lie still and stop fussing, will you?' she instructed as he wriggled again. 'Upper trapezius, upper trapezius fibres, lower trapezius...' She counted off the muscles of the back—or at least, all those she could remember from her training days—her fingers pressing firmly into James's muscular shoulders and his pale, freckly skin.

'Oooh! You've got it! Just there...*Gently,* please,' he exhaled.

'Being gentle won't help,' Abby mocked. 'Physiotherapy has to hurt a bit to be any good, you should know that.' He groaned as she dug away. 'This is a

5

medical massage, Dr Farris. We are *not* a massage parlour,' she laughed as his towel slid off again, but she kneaded the tensed-up muscle soothingly until she felt it relax under her fingertips. She could feel James beginning to relax, too. His grip on the sofa gradually gave way and he began to purr contentedly like a cat. 'See, it works,' Abby said pointedly.

'It feels wonderful. Whatever would I do without you?' He rolled over on his back, unabashed by his near-nakedness, and planted a firm kiss on her lips.

'You'd just ache a lot,' she grinned, and pecked him on the nose. He was a rugby-playing giant of a man, yet with her he was like a little boy, eager to please, anxious to be gentle. It was odd how such an easy-going character could inhabit such an uncompromisingly muscular and forceful body. Her friends at the Bentley Clinic seemed to imagine that his temperament was just as strong as his body. How little they knew! Abby thought with a smile.

James sat up on the sofa and arranged the towel around himself. His chest was smooth and he had the pallid skin of a redhead, though in fact he was brown-haired. There was a blue bruise on his left shoulder where he'd made heavy contact with a member of the opposing team at tonight's game, and he rubbed it absentmindedly. 'Something odd happened tonight, you know,' he said, puzzled. 'The full-back from the other side said he knew me. He said we'd played together at college.'

'So?' Abby curled her feet beneath her and switched the gas fire up a bit.

'I couldn't remember him for the life of me—honestly, it was like meeting a stranger.'

'Maybe he'd made a mistake. It must have been ten years since you were at college; perhaps he got you mixed up with someone else,' she suggested.

James pulled a despairing face at her. 'That's what I thought. And then he came out with all the old stories, like the time we went to Bangor and the bus broke down, and the time the entire team was sent off in the inter-varsity finals... He knew all about me and half the other guys we used to play with—but I couldn't remember him even vaguely.'

Abby stroked his bare knee as if she was comforting a child. 'It's all those bumps on the head you keep getting,' she said unsympathetically. 'You know

7

rugby's a dangerous game, and now you're beginning to find out just *how* dangerous it is!'

'You only say things like that because you care. Don't think I don't know,' he teased. 'Well, there's one way of finding out whether he's an imposter or whether I'm going mad—have you seen my photo album around?' He got up and rummaged untidily through the chest of drawers, a rather smart mahogany item that his grandmother had left him. Eventually he pulled out a tattered blue album. 'Here it is. I don't suppose you've seen this before—it'll give you a chance to find out about my mysterious past,' he added as he sat down beside her again.

Abby snuggled up against him, inhaling the fresh smell of soap and shampoo, unperturbed by his nakedness. They had been lovers since Christmas, and it had been a slow courtship by modern standards. She had deliberately held herself back from him for a long time, convinced for a while that some vital element was missing in the relationship, then finally overcome by his kindness and gentleness and obvious love for her. They were like very close, very caring friends who had moved a step further into something more exciting. But it was odd. Although those first weeks had been bliss, an oasis of delight and discovery, they seemed to have emerged from that into something deeper—something that seemed, at times and apparently only to her, to be more akin to their old, trusting friendship than giddy passion.

'Look at your hair!' She pointed to a photo of his graduation, James beaming and long-haired with his mother in a surprisingly short skirt and his father, such a conservative man, in a jacket with amazingly wide lapels. He laughed and turned on to the next page.

'Here it is, the rugger team. Now there's me...' his finger traced along the row of youthful faces...'and here *he* is! My God, I *must* have had a bump on the head. You know, I still wouldn't know him from Adam...'

'Who's this one?' Abby pointed to a dark, moody-looking man with deep-set eyes and an intriguingly twisted smile. Half his mouth seemed to turn upwards and the other half snaked down into a devilish grimace. Somehow he looked older than the rest, and she wouldn't have thought, from his apparently slim build, that he would have been much good on the rugger field. There was also something that marked him out as a man alone, a man whom one wouldn't expect to find playing team games. Perhaps that explained his enigmatic smile. Perhaps he wasn't particularly pleased to find himself one of a team.

'That one? Oh, that's Sam, Sam Malone. I don't know what he's doing in the picture. He only played a couple of times,' James snorted. 'He was very fast, could have been very good, but he wasn't keen on turning out regularly. I don't know what *he* was doing in the picture.'

'Is he the Sam who sends the postcards?' asked Abby, pleased to discover that her initial observations of the man were borne out.

'Yes, that's him.' He sighed. 'I hope he's all right.' His thoughts had obviously transported him back the ten or so years that had passed since the photo was taken. He sat gazing at the picture, running his finger from face to face as if reminding himself that it had all been real. Abby disengaged herself from under his arm and went to the kitchen to make coffee.

On the kitchen wall was a cork pinboard

covered with the bits and pieces of their life together—shopping lists, reminders of James's dental appointment, party invitations, all of them addressed to *James and Abby* as if they were to everyone's mind a permanent fixture—and Sam Malone's postcards. While she waited for the coffee to drip through the filter, Abby unpinned the postcards, which had been practically hidden by other pieces of paper. She could still remember the first evening she had come home with James. He'd cooked her a curry, and while she waited somewhat nervously in the kitchen for him to serve it, her eye had fallen on the postcards and singled them out as a good topic of conversation. Now she read them again, with a more knowing eye.

James had seemed slightly wary of saying too much about them, or about Sam, but she did know that he and Sam had been friends at medical school and that Sam had thrown in his career as a promising surgeon to join a group of surgeons in Paris—a task-force of people willing to go wherever they were needed in the world. All very romantic stuff, it had seemed, though James had made it sound crackpot. Abby wondered whether he and

11

Sam had rowed about it, and whether he would secretly have liked to do something similar. When she'd said that Sam's work sounded exciting, he'd got quite angry, telling her that Sam had always been irresponsible, had always made gestures that seemed romantic but which turned out to be of no more value than anything else. 'He's impossible,' she could hear him saying now. 'He does the most infuriating things without a second's thought for anyone else. He's totally selfish—and yet you have to forgive him. He has this incredible charisma, I suppose you'd call it. Women fall for him like ninepins. They don't realise that the last thing in the world he cares about is them...' He'd stopped with an annoyed smile on his face, as if he'd really like to have been furious with Sam but couldn't find it in himself.

Abby smiled secretly to herself and turned the cards over in her hands. The first two were just snapshots with a stamp stuck on the back of them. They seemed to be of some sort of compound. Whatever it was, it looked muddy and dilapidated and it was packed with unhealthy-looking children all smiling for the camera. On the back, in black scrawl, there was a location and she guessed, despite her rusty geography, that it had been taken somewhere on the border between Tibet and Pakistan. The message, faded after all these years, read simply, *To James. All the best for 1979, Sam.* The 1980 postcard was exactly the same.

1981's contribution had come from Bangladesh. This time it wasn't a photo but a line drawing of hills and valleys, presumably somewhere in India. After that he seemed to have changed continents, for the next three were from Africa, two from Sudan and one from Eritrea, and each of them had the same message on the back—New Year's greetings. Last year's had come from, of all places, Kabul in Afghanistan. It was a lurid picture postcard, the colours too bright to be real. And, as ever, the usual predictable message. This Christmas there had been no card. James had remarked once or twice on it, but they had been too busy falling in love and discovering each other for him to worry about a man he hadn't seen for years and whom he didn't seem to approve of anyway. Now Abby felt a twinge of guilt. Seeing Sam Malone's picture made all the difference. Suddenly, from being a vague shadow in James's past he'd become real. She could see his smile, she'd guessed at his nonconformity, and now she felt a deep stab of admiration for him. How she wished she had the courage to do the kind of thing he was doing! Or maybe he wasn't doing it any more. Maybe he'd returned to the UK, found himself some cosy niche, and decided not to send his intriguing New Year's postcards any more.

The coffee machine gave a rumbling gurgle, as if to rouse her from her thoughts, and she put the jug on the tray with the mugs and the milk. Almost as an afterthought, she placed Sam Malone's cards beside the jug and made her way back into the sitting-room. James had turned on to other pictures, other snaps and mementoes.

'Did Sam Malone ever send you a card this year?' Abby asked as she put the tray on the table and poured out the coffee. She handed him the cards with his mug, forcing him to put the photo album down.

He looked at the tatty postcards morosely. 'No, I haven't heard anything from him. Knowing Sam, anything could have happened. He might just have forgotten.'

'After all these years?' Abby asked disbelievingly. 'I was wondering whether maybe he's come home.'

'Not Sam. These—' James threw the cards back on to the table '—are to remind me that once, for a very short time, I shared his ideals. Fortunately I soon grew out of them. But Sam...Sam has to be a hero. He always wanted to be a hero—and you can't be a hero if you're a surgeon at one of the smaller London hospitals, or a GP, or a researcher, so he joined this Doctors Without Frontiers thing.' He stopped abruptly and sighed.

'And?' Abby prompted, surprised by this attack.

'Well, there's one way of being a hero, isn't there?' James pretended deep interest in his coffee mug.

'What do you mean?' She felt annoyed. Sam Malone sounded fascinating, yet all James could do was carp.

'Just think of it—a heroic doctor being killed in the course of duty. And Afghanistan would be very noble, wouldn't it? Helping the rebels in their fight against the Russian army... What more romantic way to go—and Sam could never resist a romantic gesture,' James snapped. He was tight-lipped and peeved as she'd never seen him before.

'You think he's dead?'

He shrugged, pretending not to give a damn, but Abby suspected that it was only because he *did* care that he was behaving so oddly. 'Possibly. Of course, he could have just forgotten, but I think it's unlikely. He's been trying to do something spectacular all his life, and I think he's probably succeeded.'

'Why are you being like this, James? I thought you said you were friends?' Abby protested.

'He was.' He put his mug down with a thump. 'You never knew him, Abby, so you're entitled to fantasise about him, I suppose. Those postcards have been his niggling way of reminding me of his noble deeds, that's all. I told you, he's a strange man. He's infuriating, but you can't help liking him all the same, even though you know what he's really up to. And don't ask me any more,' he said sharply.

She ignored that last order. 'You must have been very good friends. I've never seen you rattled like this by anyone else.'

James glowered at her, then smiled. 'He is quite—he *was*—quite unlike anyone I've

16

ever met. He was impossible, infuriating, and he did some terrible things. He threw all his opportunities away and he hurt a lot of people who thought they were his friends. Even so, I don't like to think of anything nasty happening to him.' He put his arm round Abby and kissed her. 'But I'm not going to let him ruin our evening together...'

'There, is that any better? It just doesn't seem to want to fall in the right direction this morning,' Abby sighed, flicking back her patient's fringe again.

Mrs Massingham studied her nurse's efforts in the mirror and pulled a face. 'No, it's still not right. I don't know how you managed to make such a mess of it, Nurse. I suppose I'll have to have the hairdresser back again. Would you arrange it for this morning?'

'Remember that the physiotherapist is coming to see you at eleven,' Abby warned. 'And I expect Mr Morton will be in before lunch just to see how you are.'

Mrs Massingham puckered her carefully glossed lips and thought for a moment. 'If Mr Morton calls and I'm having my hair done he'll have to wait a few minutes, that's all. I really *have* to be looking reasonable when my husband visits this afternoon. Oh,' she added as an afterthought, 'would you also ensure that something substantial is served with tea? I know I don't normally have anything more than a biscuit or two, but Mr Massingham will require some sandwiches.'

'No problem.' Abby picked up the menu card that her patient had filled in and made a note on the special requests section to the effect that a full afternoon tea for two was required. Patients at the Bentley had full room service, but to make use of the facility added greatly to their bill. If they gave their orders in advance and took their meals at the standard times, the luxury-hotel style service was included in their flat daily rate. 'I know that you feel as if you're fully recovered, but do take it easy,' she chided as Mrs Massingham swung her legs energetically out of bed. 'Until you've had those stitches out we need to take care. Will you be dressing today?'

'Later, when my husband's due. I can't be bothered at the moment,' the middle-aged lady replied, folding the voluminous satin pleats of her negligee around her as she sat in the easy chair and turned on the television that dominated the corner of the large room, with its queen-sized bed and reproduction furniture. Schools programmes and Ceefax flickered on the screen. Then Mrs Massingham pressed the button for the Bentley's private video channel and the familiar face of Clint Eastwood appeared. 'I think I'll watch this. Let me know when I can expect the hairdresser,' she instructed. Abby picked up the tray containing the few medical instruments she'd brought with her, checked quickly to make sure that the cleaning staff had done their duty and taken away the breakfast things, and took her leave.

The corridors of the Bentley Clinic, one of London's most modern and prestigious private hospitals, were wide and carpeted, with solid oak doors shielding its patients from any intrusion from the outside world. The only reminder that this was a hospital and not a hotel were the green lights above each door, which were illuminated when a patient required a nurse.

There were no such things as wards at the Bentley. Instead there were floors, each containing ten rooms and served by four nurses and the cleaning and catering staff. On alternate floors dwelled a Sister, who kept a watchful eye over her own domain and the floor below. Privately Abby thought that being a Sister here was a soft number. All the staff at the Bentley were SRNs with several years' staff experience behind them—experience on crowded NHS wards. They didn't need the kind of supervision that a young and inexperienced team, consisting largely of students, required, so Sister was really just there to greet patients, make her daily rounds, and liaise with the doctors and surgeons who had patients on her floors. Very rarely did she have to get her hands dirty.

Abby slipped behind the polished oak counter that divided the nurses' section of the floor from the patients'. Visitors and patients arrived in a swift lift, accompanied by soft strains of classical music. It decanted them in the waiting area by the nurses' station, where they were signed in and shown to the appropriate rooms. All the nurses had remarked how strange it was that there were so few visitors. Bearing in mind the fact that there were no restrictions on visiting hours, some of their patients had no callers from one day to the next.

Behind the oak counter, which was supposed to be staffed at all times, but invariably wasn't, there was a small lobby with four further doors. One housed the nurses' kitchen and duty room where they seemed to spend a great deal of time between attending to patients. The second led to toilets and a shower, with lockers for their belongings, the third into a prep room with its sinks and stacks of sterile supplies in glass-fronted cabinets, and the fourth into the sluice, with autoclave and other high-tech paraphernalia. There was a laundry chute for whizzing dirty linen down to the basement, and a walk-in cupboard stocked with duvets and bedspreads. And everything, just everything, from the studded plastic floors to the walls to the taps and doorknobs and chairs and cupboards, was in dazzling arctic white, so cold and hygienic that for her first week at work Abby hadn't been able to stop shivering.

She clunked into the sluice and placed the used kidney dish in the steriliser, the dressings in the furnace and the thermometer in a disinfectant bath. Then she went back to the desk, where Jenny

21

Hall, one of her friends, was filling in a set of notes.

'Had Mrs Massingham's bath been cleaned?' asked Jenny without looking up.

'Yes, I think so. Problems?' Abby filed her patient's menu card in the special rack, which would be collected soon so that the kitchens could begin work, and with a blue marker filled in details of Mr Massingham's teatime visit on the white visitors' board that was hung behind the counter. If they knew he was coming, someone could be on the lookout for him.

'The cleaners have been taking short cuts again. Sister found a tissue left under Mrs Worthington's bed and taps unpolished in most of the bathrooms. She's going to have a crackdown.' Jenny looked up and grinned. 'I'm about ready for a cup of coffee. How about you?'

Abby nodded. 'I've just got to call the hairdresser and see if he can come and do Mrs M's hair this morning, then I'll join you.'

As she entered the duty room, where the other nurses had gathered for their morning break, Abby experienced yet again that faint stirring of absurd surprise which always hit her when she saw the Bentley's uniform being worn *en masse.* The Bentley's administrators had decided to turn the clock back—which was why its nurses were clad in old-fashioned uniforms of starched pillowcase hats and equally starchy aprons over wide blue and white striped dresses. When she'd come for her interview she'd been told by Mr Pringle and Sister Bradshaw that the Bentley was to be as modern as tomorrow, but with plenty of time for yesterday. Abby smiled to herself; here they were, looking like the best-dressed nurses of 1947, in an ultra-modern setting. Still, the patients liked the traditional look, and that was all that counted.

Jenny raised her mug of coffee. 'We have cause to celebrate, ladies. Mr Finlay is leaving us today!'

There was a muffled cheer from everyone. Mr Finlay was a pushy American businessman who had been taken ill while on a business trip to London. He'd spent the past ten days running his business from his bed, jamming the switchboard with his calls, demanding secretarial help and receiving a succession of visits from bankers and wheeler-dealers. He'd even had a computer terminal installed so that he could keep track of the markets. And because he wasn't a willing patient he had done nothing but complain; about the food, even though it was prepared by a chef who had been tempted away from a top hotel, about his treatment, which was just about the best he could have got anywhere in the world, and the cost of everything. He'd been Jenny's patient, and he'd made her life hell. Although Carol Grogan and Abby had rallied round and tried to take some of the pressure off her, it had been a difficult couple of weeks.

It hadn't been helped by the fact that they'd been a nurse short for a few days, but only yesterday the replacement had arrived—and seemed to be taking to the Bentley like a duck to water, Abby thought.

'These uniforms are so nice, aren't they?' she was saying now to Carol. 'My last place had gone over to the new polyester dresses and cardboard caps, but it's so much more traditional here. I think it's lovely—so feminine and classy. Like dressing up to go to a party!'

'You wait until you've had a week or two of it. I sometimes feel as if I'm in a fashion show,' laughed Carol. She was a sensible Scottish girl and had been at the Bentley since it had opened a year ago. Compared to that, Abby was a newcomer. She'd started just after Christmas, mostly at James's instigation, because James wasn't keen on the work that she had to do and the hours that she had to put in at Highstead. He quite regularly moonlighted at the Bentley, doing routine operations—mainly joint replacements and treating complex fractures, which he was specialising in. Having seen the working conditions and questioned the nurses about their pay and hours, he'd persuaded Abby to apply for a position here. It wasn't without much heart-searching that she'd agreed—and now she regretted it. But how could she tell James, who seemed to share the new nurse's feelings about the classy uniforms and wealthy patients, that she was longing to get back to the overcrowded wards of Highstead, with their shortages of staff and scruffy surroundings? How could she admit that she longed for the vile flower-patterned curtains and matiness of Men's Medical? Once or twice she'd tried to tell him that the Bentley's thick carpets and lifts piped with 'musak' oppressed her—but he wouldn't listen, wouldn't hear of it.

'It's just marvellous to have so many people around,' the new girl, Emma, was twittering. 'It was such a strain at the last place I was at.' She pulled a hurt face as if she was looking for sympathy. 'I can remember the first day I qualified as a staff nurse and arrived on the ward to find that I was running it all on my own, with just a couple of students.'

'The NHS may be harder work,' Jenny chipped in, 'but I wouldn't agree that it was more of a strain. You haven't been here long enough yet, but you'll soon learn what I mean. It's very difficult being a cross between a nurse and a chambermaid, which is what most of the guests seem to think we are. If they were seriously ill they'd be more interesting to nurse, but most of them are in here for simple stuff that doesn't take long. They tend to treat it a bit like a holiday rather than a stay in hospital, and because they're paying so much they feel free to nag and complain as much as they fancy.'

Emma raised a curious eyebrow to Carol. 'It sounds as if she's in the wrong job, doesn't it to you, Carol?'

'Jenny and Abby have only been here a few weeks,' Carol said in her gruff

Highland fashion. 'And we've had some real terrors in during that time, so I can't really blame them for feeling fed-up.'

'On an ordinary ward everyone *has* to rub along together, and the nice people make up for the difficult ones,' Abby philosophised into her coffee cup, secretly pleased to hear that Jenny was as disappointed by the Bentley as she had been herself. 'And because it's an open ward people tend to behave themselves. If they shout at a nurse or have the TV too loud everyone knows who the troublemaker is. Here, with all these thick doors and carpets, the patients can be as rude and as difficult as they like and no one knows what's going on. Most of the patients don't even meet, so perhaps they can be forgiven for thinking that they're the only person on the corridor and that they can demand all our attention. They can't make that mistake on an ordinary ward...'

The phone rang to warn Carol that one of her patients was on his way down from theatre. He was a middle-aged executive who'd come in to have a minor orthopaedic operation on his wrist. He'd been playing too much squash and had developed a bone lesion. With luck he would be able to walk out of the Bentley, bandaged but comfortable, tomorrow. Until he came out from the anaesthetic, however, it was Carol's job to sit with him and observe his vital signs. The other nurses on the floor would care for her patients until Mr Laurence could safely be left on his own. 'Jenny, I'll be an hour or so with him. Could you see Mr Mortimer up at eleven-thirty? The notes for Mrs Barber are ready.' Jenny nodded and Carol went out to the lift area to receive her comatose charge. It was a nuisance that the Bentley didn't stretch to a proper recovery ward, Abby thought. In most modern theatres patients were monitored until they began to show signs of consciousness in a special ward near the operating theatre. The Bentley, being small and exclusive, didn't run to such facilities.

'Will you give me a hand lifting Mrs Rennie?' asked Jenny, putting her mug in the sink. 'I need a spare pair of hands to change her dressings. It'll only take ten minutes.'

Abby checked her fob watch, dangling above her left breast. 'We've got fifteen minutes before Sister's due and I've still got to make Mr Elton's notes up. We'd better be quick.'

'The tray's ready—come on!' With a giggle, they dashed out to the prep room to collect it. 'You know, I think that new girl's in for a shock if she thinks she's in for an easy time here,' Jenny commented as they collected the sterile tray, covered with its autoclaved cloth, and pushed the trolley down the corridor. 'In fact it makes me mad that she looks on it as a soft option. We're just as busy as we would be on an ordinary ward, because it takes so long to do things—like having to push this bloody trolley across thick carpets,' she swore, as the trolley, its wheels skewing in the pile, veered off course.

Abby laughed. 'It's just the grouchy patients getting to us, that's all!'

'Do you know what *I* think?' Jenny paused with her hand on the knob of Mrs Rennie's door. '*I* think that working at the Bentley is bad for our health!'

It was sleeting when Abby finished her shift and set off home—or to James's flat, which she supposed *was* her home these days. She wondered briefly whether to call in at the flat behind Highstead Hospital, where she still kept on a room. Quite why she hadn't given it up when she'd moved in with James she didn't know. Some spark of independence insisted that she have a bolt-hole to go to occasionally; she shuddered, and it wasn't just the freezing temperature and the sleet in her hair that made her shiver. Sometimes when she looked at James she found herself wondering just how long their life together could go on. And just lately he'd begun to irritate her with silly little things. She loved him dearly, but for the life of her she couldn't imagine being with him for the next thirty or forty years. While she had been working at Highstead, her room in a flat occupied solely by nurses from the hospital had been a pleasant refuge; a place to gossip and relax away from James. When he went away playing rugger with the Highstead team she spent her weekends there for company. She'd felt the need to retain part of her old life—but now all that was slipping away, what with the Bentley and James's increasing possessiveness.

It was only four-thirty and yet it was pitch dark. How she hated English winters! Maybe she'd hand in her notice at the Bentley and apply for a job working in Saudi Arabia or America. Plenty of sunshine and better pay... Her thoughts of sun and sand seemed to keep out the worst of the cold as she climbed the hill to the mansion building in which James had his flat. The place had been tarted up in the last year or so; Highstead was fast becoming a fashionable place to live and James often boasted about how the flat's value had increased by nearly a hundred per cent in the time he'd owned it. The communal entrance vestibule, once open to the public, was now guarded by a hefty brass lock and an elaborate entryphone system allowed callers to be vetted before they were allowed in. Once in, the hallway boasted a couple of smart chairs, a gilt-framed mirror, a small console table and a silk flower arrangement. The idea was to make the place appear smart and give anyone waiting a pleasant spot to sit down in—but no one ever used it and somehow it always looked a little sad and deserted.

Today, though, one of the chairs *was* occupied, and by a most unusual-looking figure who seemed to be asleep. He was dressed in a heavy dark grey overcoat and a dark fedora hat pulled well down, like a refugee from *The Third Man* or some other forties film. His face was turned away, so Abby couldn't get more than a rough idea of his age or what sort of person he was. Perhaps he was drunk, she thought ungenerously. Should she call the caretaker and have him thrown out?

He had a dark, almost emaciated look and she noticed the large, well-worn grey canvas bag next to the chair. Perhaps he was one of the London homeless, a dosser who'd somehow managed to get himself in and was enjoying the warmth of the mansions' central heating... She checked herself. He didn't look grubby or dangerous and he wasn't doing anyone any harm. James might have him chucked out, but *she* wouldn't wish anyone on the streets in such weather. She crept past him and up the stairs that led to the flat and as she went by she heard a long, wheezing breath, like a rattling sigh. He couldn't be well, she thought with a twinge of conscience. But she brushed it aside and went on up.

With the lamps in the sitting-room on and some Mozart on the stereo, the flat was a haven of warmth and comfort. Abby slipped out of her uniform into jeans and a baggy pink mohair sweater. She let her hair down and gave it a few dismissive strokes of the brush. Up or down it was a nuisance; if James wasn't so keen on it she might just go and have it all chopped off.

She'd just made a pot of tea and was settling down to read the paper when there was a knock on the door. Mindful of the man sleeping in the hallway downstairs, she opened it warily. Maybe he hadn't been asleep after all. Maybe he'd followed her to see which flat she went into. Perhaps he knew she was alone. A shiver of apprehension went through her as she opened the door a crack.

It *was* him. He stood propped against the wall opposite, and as she pulled the door back he lurched forward and clutched the frame for support. She tried to shut it, but stopped when she realised that his fingers would be trapped. There was a long pause, in which she took in his tanned face and dark, deep-set eyes. He had a nasty-looking scar, pale and silvery, coming down from one ear to his jawline, and instinctive professional interest made her wonder how he'd done it.

'What do you want?' She tried to sound both encouraging and firm. She'd dealt with many a drunken troublemaker at Highstead and knew that defensive reactions only provoked them. The man stood looking at her, his dark eyes confused, and Abby felt something uncomfortable stirring in the back of her mind. He was familiar for some reason. She'd met them before, these black eyes. But who was he?

'I'm looking for James Farris,' he said, and his voice was deep and slightly wheezy. It was obviously something of an effort for him to talk, and Abby pulled back the door and watched him sway over her. He was tall, very tall, and very thin too. In fact it didn't look as if he had strength enough in him to be dangerous. All the same, he could hardly be called a regular sort of visitor.

'James lives here, but he's not in at the moment.' Should she ask him to come in and wait? Abby thought wildly. And if he promptly mugged her and burgled the flat she wouldn't have a leg to stand on, a warning voice cautioned. As they stood there, he looming gauntly over her, she saw him begin to pale under the tan. His lips had a white line around them and gradually took on an unhealthy blue tinge. He shut his eyes and screwed them up tightly, then brought his hand, long-fingered and rough, to his mouth.

'I'm going to have to use your bathroom,' he muttered indistinctly, and before Abby could stop him, he pushed past her into the hall. 'Where the hell is it?' he asked, and she saw his body begin to slump as he went into a spasm. He was going to be sick! Instinctively she grabbed him by the arm and pulled him to the bathroom door. He seemed almost too weak to walk and she found herself opening the door and hauling him in. His hand was clamped tightly over his mouth. With the other he clutched the basin. He waited; the spasm seemed to pass and a little colour came back into his white lips. 'Get out of here and leave me to it,' he ordered in a surprisingly firm voice. Abby hesitated. He leaned back for a second and took his hat off. His hair was very dark and very short. Again she felt a niggling feeling that she ought to know him from somewhere. He turned to her, and she could see that he was having trouble focusing his eyes. The tell-tale white line was showing around his lips again. 'I told

you to get out,' he said icily. And
then he clutched the basin again, as if
in no doubt that this time she'd obey
his command.

Totally confused, Abby did so. There
was something about him, even when he
was about to throw up, that required
obedience. Like some of the starchier
and more effective doctors she'd worked
under. She went to close the front door
and found the grey kitbag outside, its
leather handles tatty and about to go
at the seams, and before she'd thought
what she was doing she'd brought it in.
Who this man was, or what he was
doing here, she had no idea. But he
wasn't drunk—there wasn't the faintest
whiff of alcohol about him—and he wasn't
well. What was more, he knew James.
She couldn't chuck him out. There was
the sound of retching and running water
from the bathroom. Then, as she stood
there puzzling what to do, everything went
quiet.

'Are you all right?' Abby tapped on
the bathroom door, but there was no
reply. She pushed the door and felt a
weight against it. She shoved harder and
there was a pained groan from inside,

but at least it opened a few inches. She peered round. He was slumped on the floor, his face wet, his legs crumpled beneath him.

'Move over,' she instructed. Nothing happened. She pushed again.

He swore, and she heard the rattle in his breath. 'I told you to leave me alone. Just five minutes, that's all I need...' He trailed off and Abby saw his head roll to one side. He was seriously ill, she could see that from here. She pushed again and managed to slip through the gap, carefully climbing over his legs. He wore jeans and heavy brogue-style shoes that had seen much better days. He muttered something but didn't—or couldn't—open his eyes. Abby reached into the airing cupboard and found a small towel. She ran some warm water in the basin, dipped the corner of the towel into it, then knelt and gently washed and dried the stranger's face. His chin and jaw were bristly and his cheekbones were starkly defined. He sighed as she touched him, but said nothing, just scowled slightly.

His skin was hot and dry now. She propped up his head and tried to straighten him, and although he still said nothing she knew her interference annoyed him. Taking his wrist, she sat quietly timing his pulse against the second hand of her watch. His pulse confirmed his general weakness; it was sluggish. She looked up from the watch to find him regarding her with a strange smile on his face. His eyes were glittery with fever, so black and inscrutable she felt almost hypnotised by them. Suddenly she felt quite grateful that, whoever he was, he was ill and at a disadvantage. Fit and well, he'd be overpowering. Everything about him was slightly intimidating, from his height to his manner of dress; from the way he ordered her around before practically passing out, to the air of unfettered sexuality that oozed from him. She'd nursed some good-looking men in her time, but never had she found someone so physically challenging. He'd barged in, thrown up in her bathroom and passed out without so much as a by-your-leave...and all she could think about was the sexy way his mouth curved and the devastating lift of his eyebrows. She could feel the bones of his wrist as she held it lightly, and something like electricity seemed to be flowing through them to her.

'Well, what's your diagnosis?' he asked, and there was a sarcastic edge to his voice. He pulled his hand away and sat himself upright.

'You've got a fever and a weak pulse. I think you're dehydrated,' she said as steadily as she could.

He nodded nonchalantly. 'Real technical stuff, eh?' He made it sound as if she was totally stupid.

'I'll get the thermometer,' she muttered, getting to her feet. 'Stay where you are.'

'I'm not going anywhere, I assure you.' He gave her a cynical smile, a smile that went up on one side and down on the other, and Abby felt her memory start with shock. She bent to look at him again. He was much thinner, and he was older too. But there was still that burning defiance, that overpowering look of complete independence from the rest of the world.

'You're Sam Malone, aren't you?' she asked simply.

He tipped his chin up and looked at her with such implacable calm that she wondered if she'd made a mistake. 'So James did remember me,' he murmured wonderingly. And then he passed out.

39

CHAPTER TWO

Abby sat on James's side of the bed and watched Sam Malone sleep. He looked so peaceful. Who would have guessed from looking at him his abrasive and defiant nature? When she'd seen that old photo of him and James had gone on about him being an impossible kind of person she hadn't been able to believe it. What had he said? That he'd never settle down; that he wanted to be a hero; that women adored him though they didn't mean a thing to him. The last memory made her start. Sam Malone had the kind of devil-may-care looks that bowled maidens over, but from her brief encounter with him she knew James was right. He was the kind of man who'd go through life alone because an attachment to a woman would complicate things. From what James said he was a medical idealist—and she felt a twinge of rapport with him, because just at the moment, with the way things were at the Bentley, she felt like giving it all up

40

and doing something deserving too.

Sam Malone groaned in his sleep and rolled over towards her. His hand brushed her leg and she moved quickly away, collecting the mug in which she'd made a milk and egg concoction for him to wash down his pills. He'd had typhoid, he said, and then malaria. And then in Nairobi he'd gone down with food poisoning. No wonder he was so thin! He'd insisted that they wait until James got home before deciding what to do.

Abby picked up the phone and dialled Highstead. It was nearly half past five. James could be home at any time and she wanted to prepare him. 'He's gone over to the Bentley to do a kneecap,' Barney Morton told her crossly when she finally got through to Theatres. 'He said he'd be through at about eight, I think. Hasn't he called you?'

'No, I don't suppose he's had time,' Abby explained, and hung up. The surgeons didn't like being disturbed in their sittingroom by girl-friends calling to find out the whereabouts of busy medics. It had been all right while she was a nurse there; she'd just been able to go along, knock quietly on the door and take a peep inside. Now she was an outsider, and she was treated as such. And senior surgeons, like Barney, didn't enjoy having to talk to her as the partner of one of their number. Just because she was involved with James, they seemed to imply, it didn't mean that she was anything more than just a nurse.

Would Sam Malone be able to hold out until eight? she wondered. He should really go into hospital now, where he could have a proper eye kept on him. She feared he was badly dehydrated and needed a saline drip...

When she returned to the bedroom he was lying on his back with his eyes open. He'd pushed the duvet down almost to his waist and she could see the sweat glistening on his exposed chest. Although he was so thin his muscle tone was good; she'd noticed that as she'd helped him to undress, much to his chagrin. His ribs poked out alarmingly, but his arms were steely strong and his pectorals were well developed. Now she tried not to show too much interest in his hairy chest.

'Drink this. You're burning up, but at least you're sweating,' she said firmly, holding out a large tumbler of water. 'It's boiled and it's at blood heat,' she assured him as he looked at it without interest. 'It won't be too much of a shock to your system.'

He raised himself a few inches, and she set the glass down before slipping her arm behind his shoulders and holding him up. With the other hand she passed him the glass and helped hold it to his lips.

'I don't need this damn Florence Nightingale act,' he snapped, pushing her hand away. The water slopped over the rim. Abby made sure he was holding the tumbler before she reached around for some tissues and mopped him. Her fingers burned on his bare skin.

'Don't flatter yourself,' she said, trying to sound disdainful despite the fact that her fingers were trembling and her heart pounding as she held him. 'It's not an act, and I couldn't give a damn what happens to you. I just don't want you dying on the premises, that's all.' And she dug her nails into his bare back.

He drained the glass and handed it to her. 'In that case I'd better have some more, hadn't I? And put two teaspoons of salt and one of sugar in it this time.'

Abby pulled her arm out from behind him and let him collapse uncomfortably on the pillows. She should have thought of a saline-dextrose combination herself, she knew with annoyance. One of the simplest solutions in the world, yet it had saved thousands of lives already simply by keeping the body supplied with vital salts and sugars. When she returned to the bedroom he was feeling around under the covers.

'You ordered it, now you can drink it,' she said, placing it unceremoniously on the bedside table.

'Yes, Nurse,' he retorted sarcastically. Now he was warmer and had had fluids the rattle seemed to have left his lungs. He was also more aggressive and more difficult. From under the duvet he pulled her nightdress. She owned four nighties. Three of them were Laura Ashley ones, high-necked and long-sleeved and guaranteed not to shock the most prudish Victorian matron. The fourth, James had bought her for Christmas. It was made of oyster satin and trimmed with cream lace, and although it wasn't quite as revealing as the sort advertised in the small ads of Sunday newspapers it was not very substantial. It was this garment that Sam Malone drew out and threw down on the bed. He looked at her and watched the colour rise in her cheeks. Then his hand went under again. She saw him ferreting around on the other side of the bed and he came up with James's blue and white striped pyjama bottoms.

He gave her a look of false puzzlement and knitted his brows for a second or two.

'You've put me in your bed,' he said slowly and deliberately, as if it had taken him an age to work it out.

'It's the only bed we've got, apart from the sofa in the study,' Abby protested, crimson.

'It's a very nice flat. I imagine property round here is expensive.' It was a snide remark, jealous and cutting. Sam Malone looked at the nightie. She tried to reach over and take it from him, but he stopped her, grabbing her by the wrist with one hand while he picked it up with the other. The satin spilled out over his fingers and he stroked it appreciatively, then looked her straight in the eye. It was a provocative, almost insulting gesture. 'It's a long time since I saw anything as nice as this,' he said softly, drawling over the words and fixing her with that sardonic look. 'I'm

45

just trying to imagine you wearing it—or not wearing it.'

Abby wanted to slap him round the face, because she knew exactly what he was doing. He was mentally stripping her. He licked his lips. 'I must say,' he said slowly, 'that James has done exceptionally well for himself. I'd never really have thought it—but then he always did what was expected of him. How long have you been married?'

Abby started. Somehow his insolent behaviour was all the worse if he believed that they were married. That he should come here and insult James's *wife* in this way...! And yet despite her instinctive desire to hate him, she wondered why he found it necessary to behave so badly. Why did he dislike her, and James, so much that he had to humiliate her like this? 'We're not married.'

'Oh, I see!' He ran his hands over the satin and lace, and Abby felt her flesh respond as if she'd been wearing the nightgown. 'Lucky old James.' His lids narrowed as he looked at her again. 'I wouldn't mind being in his shoes—and I'm already in his bed, aren't I?'

'Look, Sam, it's *got* to be hospital.' James was insistent. Abby stood outside the bedroom, unwilling to go in again. 'We can't supervise you here. Highstead's the best place.'

'I don't need supervision,' growled Sam. 'I don't want your girl-friend practising her caring skills on me, thank you. All I want is for you to put me up on your sofa for a week or two while I put on half a stone and get my strength back.'

Abby felt the bruise around her wrist where his fingers had grabbed her. It wasn't strength he needed, she thought. James had been stunned and thrilled to find Sam in his bed when he got home. He hadn't sensed the atmosphere in the flat, nor had he expressed surprise when Abby absented herself as soon as she could. If he knew the truth—that she couldn't bear to be in the same room as Sam Malone—he'd be hurt, she was sure.

'Why did you come *here?*' she asked sharply, going into the bedroom and trying not to look at the visitor, who was lying nonchalantly across the bed as if it was his.

'Come on, Abby! Sam and I have been friends for years, you know that. He's the one who sent all those postcards.' James looked surprised at her unaccustomed coolness.

'Yes, I know. I just wondered why he didn't think to call you or make arrangements.'

'Because as far as I was concerned I wasn't coming back to Britain.' Sam sounded amused at this bickering. 'I was due to be transferred to Ethiopia in January. Before I could go there I had to go to Nairobi for an orientation course—so that I could find out what had been going on, what the situation was and what my part in the project would be. And while I was there I went down with salmonella, which knocked me out. In view of the fact that I'd had typhoid last year, and malaria, they packed me back home, as they thought, for six weeks. They didn't ask if I had anywhere to go, they just put me on the first plane to Heathrow.'

'And you don't have any family?' asked Abby, eyeing him coldly.

'Abby! He's welcome here.' James was shocked.

Sam cast her a knowing glance. 'It's okay, James. She's had a lot to put up

48

with this afternoon. She doesn't want an invalid in her bed.'

'I don't care, you'll go into hospital for a few days until everything's under control and then you'll come back and stay here with us. We've got a spare room to put you up in,' James insisted. 'I'm going to call Ian Harvey and get you into Men's Medical. He'll be interested to have some tropical diseases. We don't get many in Highstead.' And, casting a disbelieving glance in Abby's direction, he went out to make the call.

'You'd better put some clothes on.' She threw Sam his tee-shirt and sweater and the jeans he'd been wearing when he arrived. Why she was acting so badly she didn't know. All she did know was that Sam's taunts seemed even worse when James was there. James looked so solid and young and naïve next to this tall, saturnine man who just lay there and answered everything with a few glib words. He was condescending in his manner, as if he was some homecoming hero—just as James had said he wanted to be. And when he looked at her with that lazy, knowing expression she could happily have murdered him.

'You're not going to help me get them

49

on?' he taunted. 'Come on, you helped me take them off.'

'That was before I knew what a bast...' Abby bit back the word. 'That was before I knew what a troublemaker you were. I don't care what you think of me, Sam, but don't you dare do or say anything to hurt James while you're here.'

'And why should I want to do anything like that?' He looked at her with what appeared to be genuine surprise.

'I don't know. I don't know quite what went on between you two all those years ago,' Abby heard herself saying. 'But whatever it was, you made a great impression on him. He admires what you've been doing and he'd be shocked if he knew what you've been saying today.' She looked at him, and he saw the confusion in her eyes.

'You are sweet, you know.' He touched her face with the rough tips of his fingers. 'Fancy being so protective! I'm impressed. You're like a cat protecting some poor little kitten.' Abby drew back and watched his eyes glaze over as another thought crossed his mind. 'Or perhaps there's more to it than that. Perhaps you're on to a good thing here. I mean—' he gestured around

50

the room. It was comfortably furnished; there was even a small TV for watching the late-night movie in bed. 'I wonder. They say that lots of girls go into nursing with the intention of catching a doctor, don't they? Maybe it's *me* who should be getting protective towards James.'

'Don't you dare! We're perfectly happy —or we were until you arrived. Why can't you go back to someone else and make a nuisance of yourself there?'

'Because my family are in America and a flight there, right now, would finish me off. Besides,' he shrugged, pulling on his clothes, 'I want to do some work while I'm here. Do a bit of research, try to get some funds going for a project I've got in mind. And for that I need to be in London. James was the only person whose address I had. So that's why you found me on your doorstep. I charmed your caretaker into letting me wait...'

Abby nodded her head knowingly. She could see it all. Yes, he *would* be charming if he wanted something badly enough. He'd do anything to get his own way. And it looked as if right now he wanted to split herself and James up.

'Come on, Abby! Why aren't you giving

the poor chap a hand?' James breezed back into the room and looked at her disapprovingly.

'She was just telling me what a good doctor you are and what a tremendous amount you're earning. And how well you look after her,' Sam added maliciously.

'She can do that later,' muttered James, bending to pull socks over Sam's bony toes. On the floor, head bent, he missed his friend's wink and his girl-friend's appalled grimace.

Ten minutes later they made their way downstairs to the car. Sam was wrapped in his greatcoat and hat as before. Abby carried a plastic bag containing a pair of James's pyjamas, toothbrush, washing kit and a lurid paperback, picked up in a foreign airport, which she had selected specially because she felt that Sam would hate it.

James left them in the hall while he went to bring the car round. Sam sat down on the chair he had occupied earlier. There was a long, awkward silence. 'I hope you soon feel better. You'll be well looked after at Highstead,' Abby told him.

'I'm sure I will—though I don't need to go. I know more about what's wrong with me than they do.' Abby found it hard to believe, looking at his tough, ungrateful expression, that he was a responsible doctor, a man who had spent years of his life living rough, endangering himself to help other people.

'You work at Highstead, I suppose?' he asked casually. 'You *are* a nurse, aren't you? I distinctly detected the caring touch.'

'Yes, I'm an SRN,' Abby admitted. Why did she feel cagey about adding that she nursed at the Bentley? She felt furious with herself. She and James had put themselves out for this man and he'd done nothing but complain and insult them. What the hell did his opinion matter to her? 'I'm not at Highstead. I moved after Christmas to a new place—not far from here, near Regent's Park.' Sam just looked at her blankly. 'Look, I'd like us to be friends,' she continued weakly, 'for James's sake if nothing else. And we seem to have started off on the wrong foot for some reason.'

'How touching!' His tone contradicted the words and she felt his eyes raking her up and down. 'The problem is, I don't know if we *can* be friends, Abby. I have a certain reputation to keep up—and I'm not the kind to smooth things over simply for the sake of keeping the peace.'

Through the glass of the doors they could see James sliding up the pavement. Sam stood up and reached for the carrier bag in Abby's hand. 'Oh, there's something that slipped my mind. I'm afraid I've got lice. I didn't have time to treat them in Nairobi. And I've been using your pillows.'

James roared with laughter. 'Don't worry about it. God, you're just as unpredictable as ever! It doesn't matter, Abby can deal with it.'

But it *did* matter, Abby thought as she heaved the bedclothes off the bed and bundled the pillows into a black plastic sack, ready for proper cleaning. Sam Malone had only been in the country a few hours and already he'd managed to come between them. He was a part of James's past—a somewhat mysterious part of it—and she was being excluded, because for some reason Sam didn't like her. He had insulted her, he had questioned her relationship with James—and he had even infested their bed. And with a terrible sinking feeling, Abby knew it was only going to get worse.

'Why don't you go and visit him? He doesn't know many people over here and he's only getting bored and difficult.' James paused to chew another forkful of chicken casserole.

'We don't get along—I've told you. I don't know why you can't sense it. When you came in the other night you must have noticed the atmosphere.' Abby was on the defensive. As far as James was concerned, her refusal to go and visit Sam, who'd been in hospital for three days now and wasn't due out for another three, was irrational.

'That's rubbish!' he protested now. 'Ouch!' His hand flew to his jaw. 'My cheek's still numb and I keep chewing it.'

'Poor thing.' Abby leaned across the table and kissed him on the nose, hoping it would distract him from talking about Sam. All they *ever* seemed to talk about these days was Sam. 'You should have looked after your teeth better and then you wouldn't have had to have so many filled at once.'

Unfortunately her tactics didn't work. After inspecting his mouth, where he'd had no fewer than six fillings, James again turned the conversation back to his friend. 'I really think you ought to go and see him, Abby. After all, when he comes out on Friday he'll be staying here and it would be better...'

'What?' Abby couldn't explain the sudden feeling of cold dread that had crept up her spine. 'He's going to stay here? Why didn't you tell me that before? I told you I didn't want him here.'

James looked indignant. 'Well, where else could he stay? He can have the study, he'll be perfectly comfortable in there. From the stories he's told me he's spent a lot of the time living very rough indeed, so I dare say our sofa-bed will seem quite luxurious.' Her stunned face still looked disapprovingly across the table. 'He's been deloused, if that's what was worrying you. And he won't be so grouchy once he's feeling better. He's a very independent guy, that's why he doesn't like people fussing over him. If you can just accept that, you'll get on like a house on fire.'

Abby shook her head. 'I don't think so. He doesn't like me.'

'What has he said to make you think that?' he asked, reaching over to help

56

himself to more potatoes.

What *had* he said? she thought, confused. She couldn't possibly tell James. James was his bosom pal—or at least, he thought of himself that way. He hadn't seen Sam's sardonic smile when he'd made his comment about James having the best of all worlds. If she were to tell him about the insulting way Sam had looked at her James would say she was just imagining it—or that Sam wasn't used to being fussed over by a pretty woman and what did she expect? At times he could be as much a male chauvinist pig as any other man. Sam was his friend, and friends stuck together. It was a sort of public school camaraderie. At parties she'd noticed how the doctors would congregate at one end of the room and share their 'manly' jokes while their girl-friends and wives were left to their own devices at the other end. When she'd first started going out with James they'd stuck together as a pair because neither of them wanted to lose each other's company for a moment. But she'd seen the curious glances of the other men and the wistful gazes of the women—and now she could see why. It was all too easy to lose a man's interest, and not just to another woman, but even to another man! James couldn't have been more excited and pleased if Miss World had come to stay. Right now, Sam was more important than her.

It was almost as if James had read her thoughts. 'You're jealous!' he crowed, throwing down his knife and fork. 'You don't like the idea of sharing me with him, do you?'

Abby pushed back her hair and leaned her arms firmly on the table. 'No, I don't think I'm jealous of him...' How could she say she didn't trust him? That there was something threatening about him and that she thought he half had it in mind to make trouble for them both? How could she tell James that his old pal didn't, from what she'd seen, like him very much? 'Just go careful with him, please, James. Seven years is a long time and he's probably changed. He's a different person. Harder, ruthless, maybe not very nice to be around.'

'I don't understand this.' James turned a bewildered gaze to the kitchen ceiling. 'Women! You're all totally irrational—and jealous! We ought to be giving Sam the time of his life, considering what he's been doing while we've been having a soft time of it, and instead of that you're complaining because I've offered him a room here.'

'*You've* fallen into his trap,' Abby retorted. 'You told me he wanted to be treated like a hero, and yet here you are making him out to be a saint, some kind of Bob Geldof. In actual fact he's nothing but self-opinionated and rude—and you choose to excuse his behaviour by calling him tough and noncomformist...'

James cut her short by standing up. 'Look, I've had a hard day of it. These fillings are killing me and I don't want to argue with you about Sam. I'm going back to the hospital to check up on a patient and then I'm going to the Sports Club for a drink. You can come along if you like, but only if you promise not to say another word about him.'

'I'll stay here and do the washing-up—and the ironing,' Abby heard herself saying bitterly before she'd given the matter any thought. She saw a flicker of real annoyance cross James's face and realised that she'd never seen it before. They'd had disagreements, but they'd never got to the stage when one of them had walked out.

'If you want to come I'll help you do

59

that later,' he said tightly. 'Come with me, and we'll pop in and see Sam and get things sorted out.'

'No. I'll go and see him tomorrow, if it means that much to you, but not now. Not after we've rowed over him.' She shook her head firmly.

'I'm sorry.' James crossed the kitchen and took her in his arms, squeezing her so tight that she could scarcely breathe. 'I'm in a foul mood because of these teeth—and it's difficult for you to understand Sam. He's always been an awkward so-and-so.' He hugged her again. 'He'll only be here for a few weeks and then we can be alone again and forget all about him. Can you put up with him for my sake?'

Abby sighed and, gritting her jaw, nodded. She would have to compromise if Sam Malone wasn't going to drive them apart. And when she was in James's strong arms she could be persuaded to do almost anything. Maybe she'd imagined those innuendoes and Sam's insolent tone. After all, he had been fairly seriously ill. And he *had* had a tough time of things, by the sound of it; that kind of life affected a man...

'All right. He can stay.'

60

James pecked her on the lips. 'You won't regret it, darling. Wait until you get to know him. Then you'll love him, just like everyone else.'

CHAPTER THREE

All was quiet on Men's Medical. A few visitors were chatting in desultory fashion to patients and from the TV room at the end of the ward came the sound of a children's programme. Abby glanced in and found half a dozen middle-aged men watching *Blue Peter*.

Sam Malone wasn't among them—but then she didn't imagine he was the kind to sit and watch television. She walked down the ward again, quite at ease in her surroundings and feeling increasingly nostalgic for the smells and sounds that she'd given up for the Bentley. At this time of the year the ward windows weren't opened, so lunch smells—fish fingers and cabbage, she knew instinctively—were still drifting on the air. And like background music to it all was the occasional squeaky thrum of a trolley, the distant mechanical grind of the lift and the echoing calls and bumps from the miles of corridor. She suddenly felt homesickness overtake her gut dread of having to see Sam. She'd trained at this hospital; she'd spent six months on this very ward! She knew how loudly the wind could moan around the corner of the building, setting up an unearthly wail that frightened patients in the night, and she knew that the hospital radio reception was dreadful up here. Why, she wondered, had she ever allowed James to persuade her to leave?

There was the sound of muffled voices from the side ward, and then June Whittaker, pink-faced and furious, shot out into the main area. 'What are you doing here?' she asked sharply, then, 'Oh, I didn't mean that to sound so rude! Sorry, Abby. But what *are* you doing here? I thought you'd transferred to the new private hospital.'

'I have,' Abby smiled. 'But I've come back here to visit someone.'

June slammed a kidney dish with an empty syringe down on to the metal trolley so hard that one of the patients in a nearby bed jumped and looked over

62

at them curiously. 'And how's it going?' June bustled around, pulling out a dressing tray for her next patient. 'Champagne and roses all day every day, I suppose.'

Abby thought she detected a hint of acrimony in the girl's voice and manner. 'No, anything but. A lot of stuck-up and difficult patients who think that because they're paying through the nose for their treatment they can do and have anything they want. I was just wishing I was back here, actually.'

June gave a hollow, disbelieving laugh. 'I suppose you want our hero.' She slammed a pair of forceps on to her tray and they bounced off, on to the floor.

'Our hero?' Abby raised an enquiring eyebrow. 'If you mean Sam Malone, yes, I do. Don't tell me you've fallen for the blarney too!'

'The ward's divided pretty evenly down the middle,' sniffed June, retrieving the forceps and chucking them into the dirty bin. 'There are those who think he's the most marvellous creature ever to stalk the earth and who can do nothing but sit on his bed all day and admire him. And then there's the rest of us who think he's the most egotistical, bloody-minded...'

'It's all right, June, I know. I'm on *your* side,' Abby said wryly. 'I'm pleased to hear I'm not the only one. James seems to think the sun shines out of—'

'*He* thinks the same thing himself,' June interrupted. 'He's in there, on his own.' She indicated the side ward. 'Mr Cunliffe was in with him until yesterday, but couldn't stand the strain.'

'Is he being *very* difficult?' asked Abby, suddenly nervous again at the thought of having to confront him.

'He doesn't want to stay in bed, but when we want him up he says he's too busy doing what he's doing to get out. He's had a row with Ian Harvey about his medication because he insists he knows best, and the librarian was down this morning because your Dr Farris went up to the library and got him a load of books he isn't supposed to have...'

Abby groaned. 'I suppose I'd better go and say hello, anyway.'

'Good luck. And if you're not out in half an hour I'll come in with reinforcements and get you.' June gave a grim smile and swept off to her next patient.

Sam was sitting on his bed wearing a white tee-shirt that made him look darker than ever, and a pair of his baggy cotton pants. The second day after he'd been admitted, James had come home to the flat with strict instructions to take in something for him to wear. Apparently Sam never wore pyjamas and was now well enough to insist on an alternative. Compared to the normal run-of-the-mill patients in their Marks & Sparks dressing gowns and Rupert Bear slippers he looked very exotic. He did not belong here, and his appearance was all part of his protest at having been admitted, Abby thought. She tried to swallow the little thread of fascination that seemed to tickle the back of her throat. He was a very attractive man, she told herself; it was natural to feel some sort of interest in him. But the moment he opened his mouth she'd quickly come to her senses, as she had done before.

He was reading and either hadn't noticed her approach or was studiously ignoring her. She coughed once, then twice. He finished the page he was on and looked up, and she was surprised to see that he was wearing glasses, large fashionable ones with thin black frames that made him look very academic and exceedingly continental. But then he'd spent the last few years working with a French-organised agency, she remembered.

'Hello.' He inserted a file card covered with notes and closed the book. It was, she noticed, one of the very best studies on modern gunshot and shrapnel wounds.

'James asked me to come and see you,' she said, trying to keep any warmth from her voice. This time *he* would have to be the one to cover the frozen ground and apologise, because she knew that if she showed herself to be too soft or forgiving he'd just take advantage of her. From her bag she took the things she'd brought for him. Orange juice, a couple of current affairs magazines and his electric razor, which had been broken and had just come back from the menders.

'Great!' he exclaimed, seizing the latter. 'I can't get a decent shave with these plastic things,' and he switched it on and began to use it. Abby, painfully aware that he hadn't greeted her or made her welcome in any way, stood and watched him. The inside of her mouth was suddenly dry. Although he pretended to be absorbed in shaving his beard, she had an uncomfortable feeling that he was also inspecting her surreptitiously—that as he moved his head and raised his chin he cast his eyes in her direction. She wondered if she should simply turn around and leave, but something held her there.

'Are you just going to stand there?' he said at last. 'Come and sit down.' He patted the edge of the bed and she noticed for the first time that the chair at his bedside was piled with books—medical books. She undid her coat and sat down as far away from him as she could get, at the other end of the bed. 'I'm catching up on my reading,' he explained nonchalantly, motioning to the tomes around him. 'I don't often get the chance to look at the latest research and technology. Oh, I forgot...' He reached over into the bedside locker and took out his wallet. 'Here you are—for the magazines and the shaver.'

A five-pound note fluttered in his fingers, and Abby felt pleased to see that his hands were still shaky. He was obviously better but still not at the peak of fitness. The knowledge made him easier to face, for some reason.

'I couldn't possibly! You're James's friend—'

'I'm not your friend, though, am I? And I bet you paid for these things.' His eyes were still the same black, still sparkling with that strange, defiant energy.

'I can't accept it. You're our guest. The very least I can do is bring you a few comforts while you're here. There's no need for you to pay your way.' His offer unnerved her, and so did his stare. Abby began to wish she'd walked out on him when she'd had her chance. His feet were next to her on the coverlet, and she noticed how sinewy they were. James's feet, pale and very slightly pudgy from the long hours he spent operating, came unbidden to mind.

'Don't worry, I can afford it. But then I expect you can too.' Sam was alert, watching her reactions so closely that Abby felt alarm bells ringing in her head. He was up to something. He was trying to make her say or do what he wanted.

'James has been telling me all about your job—and about his private work as well. It sounds very lucrative.'

Sam watched her face—her instant confusion, the teeth clenched with hostility. A stab of self-disgust that he could behave like this hit him, but he didn't let his questioning smile falter. Abby fiddled with her hair and examined the self-weave pattern on the pale green bed-cover. She was such an easy target, Sam thought. None of the hardness or calculation he'd at first imagined. She really was an innocent—like James. His unreasonable resentment of James flooded him again. Not only did James have security and wealth, but he seemed almost obscenely contented with his little life. And he had this girl. Sam's fingers itched to stroke her glorious mane of hair. Everything about her appealed to him—and not just because she was James's live-in girl-friend. That added to his frustration, of course, but Sam knew he'd have felt the same way about her whatever the circumstances.

He'd had too much harshness in his life. He needed someone like this, someone soft and kind and strong in her own way. But he couldn't have Abby. He felt the resentment tear at him again. He remembered his college days with James, when both of them had been idealistic and youthfully naïve. James had always been innocent of the real world, and he didn't know much more about it now. Sam had been older, more knowing and more sceptical. They'd made a good pair. In their final year as housemen they'd investigated the opportunities for working abroad. They'd gone to various agencies and taken short courses in tropical medicine. And then suddenly, just when everything was coming together, James's heart had gone out of it and he'd backed away, talking about getting a couple of years' experience first, of establishing himself. He'd certainly done that, Sam thought grimly.

Abby looked at him and saw that he was thinking—though of what she had no idea. Perhaps he was devising more ways in which he could get at her. She wondered for the thousandth time what she had done to offend him so deeply that he had to attack her like this. Sam focused on her again. 'What were you thinking about?' she asked quickly, hoping he'd forgotten his last comment to her.

'About my first posting. I was thinking about your job at this private clinic and about the nurse who worked at the refugee camp where I spent my first fourteen months. You haven't told me what sort of work you do. I expect your surroundings are more conducive than this.'

'They are at first glance. It's all plush suites and gourmet meals. But underneath it's not so very different from here—and it's no better to work in despite what James says. He thinks that if a place looks nice then it *is* nice, but he doesn't really appreciate how difficult a nurse's job is even in luxurious surroundings.' Abby stopped abruptly, annoyed that she'd so much as hinted that her opinion of the Bentley differed from James's. 'From what I've heard, you're not a very good patient. I'm surprised. I would have thought that with your experience you'd know how tough a nurse's life can be.'

He hit back immediately. 'I didn't want to be brought in here and fussed over like a child. And as for the bureaucracy in this place—if I don't want to eat my lunch at twelve then I won't, no matter how many nurses are sent to cajole me into it—'

'Is that the worst thing that's happened to you?' Abby snapped. She shouldn't argue with him, she knew. It would be best just to ignore him. But he was so pig-headed, so selfish! 'Do you realise the repercussions your little lunchtime stand has? Every minute a nurse has to spend standing over you she's kept away from other more important work. While you're in here moaning about the food someone else is out there in the ward waiting for a

71

bedpan with their knees crossed in agony.' He laughed at the idea, but she went on, 'Do you think June Whittaker wants to persuade you to eat? She couldn't give a damn if you miss a meal—except that if Sister or Ian Harvey find out she'll get a rocket. I would have thought that *you*, of all people, would have known better—until I met you, of course, and I began to understand just what an unreasonable person you are!' She sat back, her heart pounding. The nerve of the man! She wanted to shake him—and yet still, she couldn't quite believe he was as awful as he seemed to be. There *must* be something motivating him, making him so bloody-minded and unco-operative.

He shrugged. 'Do you seriously call this nursing?' He gestured out to the main ward, where there was a crash, as if June was secretly listening and expressing disapproval. 'This constant round of meals and bedpans and tucking in sheets? Come on, Abby, even you can do better than that.'

'I don't know what you're talking about,' she insisted.

He leaned forward off his pillows and took the lapel of her coat, pulling her closer to him. 'Let me tell you what *I* think nursing's about. It may surprise you. My first posting was to a refugee camp on the Pakistan border, designed to receive the Tibetans who were escaping the Chinese. It sounds picturesque, doesn't it?' he asked, leering at her.

Abby said nothing. She could hardly breathe when he was this close. He seemed to mesmerise her, like a stoat does a rabbit. All she could take in was the darkness of his fierce eyes and the fury that seemed to make him bristle. It wasn't that he frightened her. He was dangerous. How or why she didn't know; it was pure instinct.

'It wasn't picturesque, I can tell you. We had hardly any resources, so we had to turn the adults away and just keep the children. There were four hundred of them, and two nurses, and me, fresh out of training. We had starvation rations and one blanket between every three kids. The Tibetans don't have Western ideas of hygiene, so the place was filthy, a breeding ground for all kinds of disease.' His eyes glittered with fervour and Abby couldn't pull herself away. 'The children slept on a mud floor and the three of us in the medical team had an empty room with a concrete floor and nothing else. There was no nursing in the sense *you* mean it. Those nurses did everything. They performed operations, if necessary. They scrubbed the scabies off the kids until they screamed. They made their own diagnoses and prescribed what drugs we possessed if they had to.' He stabbed the air angrily with his fingers as he spoke. 'On my first morning there I had to do a post-mortem on a little boy who'd died the night before—and when I opened him up he'd died of worms. *Worms!*' Abby could see his hand beginning to shake as he held her coat. His grip slackened and he ran his hand across his face. 'Don't talk to me about how hard-pressed these nurses are—or you, in your private hospital. These days most nurses are little more than auxiliaries—'

'That's absolute rubbish!' Abby flashed.

'And when did you last have to use an ounce of initiative? Nurses aren't stupid and they have to have more than the average measure of dedication, yet what do they end up doing? Running around in glorified hotels serving meals and changing the occasional dressing.'

Sam's mind went back to the conditions of that first, terrible camp. It had taken him a month to get over the appalling conditions, which had hit him physically, almost like a punch on the jaw. He'd spent his first weeks there unable to believe it was really happening, convinced that sooner or later more money would be poured into the project and the daily suffering and despair would be relieved. But it wasn't—and soon he had developed the rhinoceros skin needed by anyone who was to cope in such circumstances. It didn't mean he was immune to the suffering, merely that he could bear it. But it didn't stop the anger, the resentment building in him. Every day a child died of the kind of ailment that could have been successfully treated by the average GP—of something as simple to deal with, in theory, as worms or a minor chest infection. Every day he had reflected on the difference just one more doctor, like James, would have made to the project. And every night he'd fallen asleep exhausted in his sleeping bag on the bare concrete floor of the staff quarters. He'd been too tired even to dream. When Christmas had come around he'd posted off that first card to James, hoping to stir his conscience. Much good it had done. James had settled for the good life.

Much of what he said was true, Abby acknowledged to herself. Cuts in the Health Service and the increase in technology meant that a lot of the responsibility had gone out of nursing. Oh, there were new skills to be learned, new responsibilities to be taken, but increasingly, junior nurses were taking the place of domestics and senior nurses were becoming administrators. To someone returning from the kind of conditions Sam had described, it must seem very petty. He'd slumped back on his pillows.

'I apologise for the strength of my feelings,' he murmured, but he was being sarcastic, as usual. 'No one likes to hear the truth.'

'A lot of what you say is right.' Abby tried to make it sound as if she'd heard it a dozen times before. As if his passion, his strength of feeling had meant nothing to her. If it had been anyone else she would have admitted that she'd often found herself wondering if there wasn't more than what she was doing at the moment. But this was Sam Malone, and she'd find no sympathy here. 'Unfortunately we don't all

76

have it in us to do what you do. And I don't happen to believe that simply because of what you've done over the past few years you have the right to come back and start throwing your weight around. No matter what you say, everyone in this hospital is doing a good job.'

He shook his head bitterly. Rage boiled inside him—not just at Abby, but at James and everyone else. 'You're so complacent! So long as you're all right, nothing else really matters to you, does it? James is raking it in with his private work and ignoring his waiting list here. You're wasting yourself in a private hospital arranging people's flowers nicely... You've got your flat and your car and your holidays. Pretty soon you'll have a house in the country, too. And then a couple of kids. You think you've got it all. You think you *know* it all. But in fact you know nothing, Abby. You'll never know how the majority of the people on this planet manage to survive against incredible odds. You may be able to create your own cosy little cocoon and escape all the pain and suffering, but you'll never be able to say you did anything to help solve it. And for that I despise you, you and James.'

'Don't!' Abby tried to get up, but he gripped her, and with that surprising strength she'd experienced before he pinned her down to the bed, his arm behind her shoulders forcing her face down to his. She smelled of tea roses. He'd noticed her bath oil and talc in the bathroom that first day and wondered what they would smell like, and now he knew. Simple, fresh, slightly old-fashioned. He didn't say anything, just held her there and marvelled at the natural peaches and cream of her complexion. He felt her sob. 'Don't say things like that! If it's what you think then don't come and stay with us—you'll only hurt James. He thinks he's your closest friend.' She lifted her face defiantly to him. 'I don't care what you say about me. I despise you just as much as you despise me.'

Sam's conscience pricked him. Why should he take it out on Abby when none of it was her fault? Why hurt her just because he was furious with James? Why hurt either of them when they'd done him no harm? But the urge to hit out at someone, anyone, was strong. His best revenge on James would be to seduce Abby, but something in him sensed that it would be no easy task. And anyway, he didn't want to get involved.

He released her and watched her stand up. There were tears in her eyes, tears of fury and indignation, and he felt sudden remorse. 'I didn't mean to—'

'Yes, you did,' she stopped him. 'I've got your number now, Sam. You think you're some kind of martyr and you want the rest of us to feel guilty and in awe of you because you've done something we could never do. When in fact all you are is a nasty piece of work. You can't take pleasure in anyone else's happiness, can you? You can't accept the rest of us for what we are. But just try listening to yourself for once and you might realise how smug you sound!' She picked up her bag, which had fallen on the floor. 'When James told me about you I thought you sounded terrific. I wanted to meet you because I thought that anyone who'd done what you had would really be worth meeting. What I hadn't realised was that everything you do is for yourself, not for anyone else. In fact you're the most selfish person I've ever met.'

'That puts me in my place, doesn't it?' he said flippantly, as if her words were just water off him. 'You sound as if you've got a guilty conscience,' he added for good measure.

But it was too late. She had walked away, off into the main ward, leaving him on his own with just his books for company. Sam picked up the report he'd been reading before, but he couldn't concentrate on it. He turned his lamp out and lay gazing at the white wall by the side of his bed.

'You can't go! I won't let you.' James stood obstinately in the doorway. 'There's no need for you to go, I told you.'

'I know you did,' Abby murmured placatingly as she began to take clothes from the wardrobe and pack them into a bag, 'but I simply can't share the flat with him. Anyway, it'll be fun for you two on your own. All boys together—it'll be like old times.'

'I don't want that, that's in the past. I want to be with you, all the time.' James came close and began to stroke her hair as it hung down her back. He pulled it out into a braid and began to plait it, his fingers smoothing her neck, enticing her. He knew just how to get round her, Abby thought ruefully, but this time she didn't melt to him.

'I know you find it difficult to believe that we don't get on, but it's true, darling,' she insisted. 'You should have heard him when I went to visit him—'

'Was he rude?' asked James, suddenly protective.

'Not rude—not really. He just doesn't like me. I suppose he resents me being here. Maybe he was hoping that he'd come back and things would be just the same as they were when he went away.' She didn't mention the strange, enigmatic sort of friction she felt when she was in Sam Malone's presence. It was almost like being hypnotised by a snake. She knew he meant nothing but ill towards her and that it was folly to have anything to do with him, yet there was something about him that disturbed her in a more worrying way. Part of her wanted to stay, wanted to find out what it would be like to have him around every day.

'It's his manner. He's probably not used to having women around,' James laughed.

'He is—he told me all about the nurses he'd worked with and how they work so much harder than nurses over here. And he had a go at me about working in a private hospital—so you'd better play down your private work if you want any peace,' warned Abby, wagging a mocking finger in James's direction.

He dropped to his knees at her side and pulled her down to sit on the bed. 'Please don't go. We're a couple and I want you here. I don't want Sam to think that it's just a flash in the pan with us.' His hazel eyes, fringed with gingery lashes, were earnest. 'Is it because we're not married? Is that why you feel uncomfortable with him?'

Abby didn't answer. Yes, she found Sam's comment when he'd discovered that they weren't married very offensive. But it wasn't really that.

'I can easily mend that situation. Will you marry me, Abby? And Sam could be best man!' He seemed pleased with the idea. 'It couldn't have worked out better, could it? Why don't we?' He kissed her firmly on the cheek. 'Say yes, please, Abby! You couldn't make me happier.'

Abby's head spun. She couldn't account for her immediate reaction which was to say no and continue packing, nor the surge of panic that rose when she thought of

Sam as James's best man. But why should she feel that way? she wondered. If there was one way of proving to Sam that his suspicions were unfounded and that *he* was the interloper and not her, it would be to marry James. And she *did* want to be James's wife... 'Sam wouldn't like it.' She tried to make it sound like a joke. 'He thinks I'm only after your money.'

'That's just his sense of humour.' James looked deep into her eyes. 'You haven't said yes yet. Don't you want me?' His strong arms crept around her and he hugged her tightly. When he held her like this she felt safe from the world, confident that, come what may, he would make everything all right. If only she could banish this one tiny, nagging voice at the back of her mind, a voice that kept saying something she couldn't understand, everything would be perfect.

'You're beginning to worry me.' He turned her face to his, made her look at him. 'What's wrong? You haven't fallen out of love with me, have you?'

'No, of course not. But Sam really wouldn't like it,' Abby sighed. 'He'll be more difficult than ever.'

'Damn Sam, it's you that I want.'

He hugged her more tightly than ever. 'Brides-to-be don't traditionally live with their husbands until the wedding, so I suppose if you moved back to your flat for a week or two it would be all right. We can get a special licence, so we won't have to wait long... You still haven't said yes,' he reminded her, and he looked so pitiful and so honest that Abby couldn't help herself. Sam Malone might be a fascinating character, but he wasn't a man to get close to. And James... Yes, she loved James in a calm, quiet, reliable way; she would never do anything to hurt him, never be disloyal to him.

'Yes, I'll marry you,' she agreed.

CHAPTER FOUR

'You're getting married? To James?' Jenny dropped her pen and it rolled off the desk and on to the floor. Abby saw her check the flicker of disbelief that hovered over her face for a moment, then she beamed. 'Oh, Abby, congratulations!'

'Thanks.' Abby shuffled and suddenly

felt a bit sheepish. She'd never really thought of herself as the type of person to get engaged. All her life she'd tended to go for the unconventional; she'd trained as a nurse instead of going to university, like the rest of her brothers and sisters. And she'd been surprised at how willingly she'd moved in with James, with barely a thought about a wedding ring. It was odd. When a situation felt exactly right the conventions didn't matter; one forgot about the formalities. Jenny was looking at her quizzically. 'What's wrong?' Abby asked. 'Do I detect a slight air of disbelief?'

'No, of course not!' Jenny laughed, then sobered. 'I was just wondering why you were standing there looking as if you were due for a trip to the dentist in ten minutes.'

'I was *not!*' protested Abby.

'Oh yes, you were. Don't tell me that now he's popped the question you don't want to marry him.' Their eyes met, Abby's slightly wary, Jenny's perceptive, and there was immediate understanding.

'It's just happened so quickly,' Abby shrugged. 'And they say that everyone gets nervous before a wedding.'

Jenny gave a snort. 'Not the day they've

been proposed to, they don't. They're over the moon for the first week, *then* the doubts start creeping in. Come here and sit down.' She pulled out the chair beside her and Abby sat willingly. She missed sharing a flat with other nurses, girls you could talk to about all sorts of things. There were some things James couldn't understand, things he laughed off as being 'women's problems'. She sometimes felt lonely, even with him there. Strange how you could feel lost, even with someone else in the room with you. Perhaps that was why she had kept on the flat, she thought, so that if things got unbearable she could run away to it.

'What do you think of James? Honestly, Jenny. I'm not going to take offence at anything you say, but I'd just like your opinion.'

Jenny screwed up her eyes in thought. 'He's a very nice, kind sort of man, from what I know of him. He's quite gentle with the patients and he doesn't have the ego that makes so many of the doctors so unbearable.'

'And?' Abby saw a light flicker on the callboard and then go out. It was after-lunch snooze time, a quiet hour between the meal and visitors. Most patients watched television or dozed, and they had no one today who needed special attention.

'Look, I've only been to your place a couple of times and I haven't worked much with him here,' protested Jenny.

'Say what you think, Jenny.'

'Well, as you're so insistent, I will.' Jenny grimaced apologetically. 'I think he's dull, Abby. I don't mean that I think he should go to discos and get involved in politics and take up a cause or anything like that. He's just...well, he's a very mild sort of man, from what I know. He seems to prefer a quiet life to any excitement. And he's a man's man, too. I don't think he finds it easy to talk to women—not to me, anyway. I just get the feeling that he's more at home with men, playing rugger, having a drink with the other surgeons, that kind of thing.' She glanced at Abby's knitted eyebrows. 'Look, I did tell you I don't know him very well.'

'You're right—at least, a lot of what you say is right,' Abby admitted slowly. 'James is a very conventional person, and I suppose that *could* seem dull.'

'He won't want you to work once you're married, will he?'

'Why not?' Abby looked up, surprised.

'I know he'd rather you'd given up nursing altogether, even when you came here. As far as he was concerned this was better than Highstead but not as good as having you at home all the time.' Jenny leaned forward and murmured conspiratorially, 'And I dare say he'll want children, too, before long.'

Abby stared at the patient file Jenny had been filling in when she'd dropped her bombshell, and silently cursed her friend for voicing all the niggling doubts that she herself had had since last night. She hadn't had any sleep. Instead she'd lain awake, James's arm around her while he snored into her right ear, and wondered what the future would bring. James was security, safety, utter reliability. If he'd been a car he'd have been a rugged family saloon, tough and roomy, but certainly no sports car. Sam Malone was one of the world's sports cars, fast, dangerous and with poor suspension that gave a bumpy but exciting ride. Maybe she should try something a bit more racy before she settled for a family saloon? She winced. At four o'clock this morning it had all made sense; now it sounded silly. Poor James. She loved him, so why was she thinking of him like this?

'I'd like that,' she said without much enthusiasm. 'I want to have children—'

'Not yet!' Jenny broke in. 'Look, Abby, you're a good nurse. You've got your heart in the right place! There are millions of girls who'd jump at James simply because of the life he can offer them, but you're not like that. You're a nurse because of what good you can do for people, not just as a job until Mr Right comes along and sweeps you off your feet. There are others who wouldn't give it a second thought—' she nodded her head to the other chairs at the counter, and Abby knew she meant the other nurses on the floor '—but...'

'All right, all right!' Abby held up her hand. 'I'm going to have to give this a lot of thought, I can see. But anyway, whatever I decide, we're having a party on Friday and you're invited.'

'An engagement party?' Jenny looked amused.

'No, a party for Sam—the one I told you about. James's friend who's—'

'The one who's come back from Africa?' Jenny's eyes glinted with interest. 'I'm

89

dying to meet him. He sounds amazing.'
Unconsciously she licked her lips and Abby
noted it. She hadn't said a lot about Sam,
and certainly nothing complimentary, but
Jenny had taken an immediate interest
in him, ignoring the critical remarks and
latching on to everything that sounded
exciting and romantic. What had June
Whittaker said? Something about the world
being divided into the half that loved Sam
Malone and the half that actively disliked
him. Well, in this particular war she and
June were on one side and Jenny and James
on the other.

'He must be a very interesting man.'
Jenny had a glazed look in her eye. 'You
never told me if he was handsome.' She
laughed. 'Come on, be truthful now, like
I was with you. Is he as good-looking as
he should be, with a reputation like his?'

Abby allowed Sam's image to flicker
for a second in front of her eyes,
before banishing it again. 'Yes,' she
said grudgingly. 'He's impossibly good-
looking—and he knows it. I warn you,
Jen, when he turns on the charm there's
no way you'll be able to withstand him.'

'Who says I'll want to?'

'Oh, you don't want to go falling for

his stories. He's...I don't think he's a very good man at heart.' A tiny pinprick of indignation stabbed Abby's heart. Why did everyone else except her and June Whittaker think Sam was the bee's knees? Why was he so horrible to some people when he could bowl others over with his effortless charm? Why, why did he have to be so nasty to her?

'He's not like James, is that what you're saying? Well, maybe you ought to allow him to charm you and give you a taste of a more exciting life,' Jenny suggested mischievously. 'Try something a bit different and see how you like it. Then you'll know whether you're making the right decision with James.'

'Jenny!' Abby looked aghast. 'You don't know the man. He's accused me of seducing James for his money, of selling out by working here...'

'I've heard you say something pretty close to that myself,' Jenny chipped in. 'You want to be careful, Abby. It's beginning to sound a bit "the lady doth protest too much". You wouldn't be so hot under the collar about him if you weren't interested in him.'

At that moment a light flickered on the

board and the bell sounded. 'It's Mrs Massingham.' Abby got to her feet. 'I'll have to go. She probably needs some help to get to the bathroom.'

'Saved by the bell, eh?' laughed Jenny. It was funny, Abby thought, as she walked briskly down the corridor, but exactly the same thought had occurred to her. Jenny was wrong, of course. Sam Malone *was* rude and pushy. He'd deliberately set out to undermine her, not like a stranger being inadvertently disturbing. Well, he wouldn't undermine her or upset her again, not now she and James were engaged. She imagined his shocked reaction on hearing the news. *That* would put him in his place!

She was so nervous she could barely get her key into the lock. Fortunately, James heard her fumbling and came to open the door. 'I'd begun to think you weren't coming,' he told her as he took the carrier bags that contained food and a couple of bottles of wine for the evening. 'Nervous?'

'Terrified,' Abby admitted. Quite why she felt as if her knees were about to give way she wasn't sure. Part of it had to do with the fact that she knew she'd have to meet Sam again. But there was, far worse than that, an unnameable dread hanging over her. 'There was no need for me to bring anything, I see,' she said as they went into the kitchen. The table was covered in bowls and plates of appetising bits and pieces and the worktops held more than a dozen bottles of wine. 'It looks lovely.' She took a deep breath. 'Where's Sam?'

'In there.' James nodded towards the sitting-room. 'He did a lot of this, actually. Come on, come and welcome him...' He went to lead her into the other room, but saw her momentary hesitation and stopped. 'Look, he's not going to eat you! You're scared of him, aren't you?' He came close and tilted her chin up so that she had to look him straight in the eye.

'Not scared of him,' Abby admitted. 'It's just that everything he says seems to be aimed at getting at me. He intimidates me.'

'It's all part of his fatal charm,' he smiled. 'First the women back off in awe, then they fall for him! We'll have to see if we can get him paired up with one of your friends this evening, won't we? Then he won't feel the need to intimidate you.' He kissed her briefly.

'Have you told him about...' Abby paused. She couldn't find the words, couldn't, for some reason, bring herself to say the fateful words 'engagement' and 'marriage'.

'No, I haven't told him that we're getting married. Or anyone else, for that matter.' James tweaked her nose teasingly. 'I thought we could make it a big surprise for everyone this evening.' Abby managed a wobbly smile. 'Come on now, come and say hello properly. After all, it'll be the first time you've met him when he hasn't been ill or in bed!'

Sam was sitting on the sofa, his head back and his eyes half closed listening to *Don Giovanni* on the stereo, and for a moment it looked such a studiedly relaxed pose that Abby wondered whether he'd had his ear glued to the kitchen wall, listening to them. He didn't seem to sense their presence for a full minute. Then he opened his eyes, saw them and rose to his feet. 'Hello, Abby.' He held out his arms to her welcomingly and James propelled her forward.

'You can kiss her this once,' he said with mock reproof, and before Abby could take evasive action, that was what Sam did. His lips came down firmly on to hers, not to her cheek or her brow, and lingered there, while his arms smoothed her shoulders caressingly. Abby stood rigid with shock and tried to ignore the spark of electricity that flowed through her veins and seemed to make her entire skin, even her scalp tingle. Sam could feel her resistance and had to fight back the urge to kiss her again, to hold her hard to him, until she unfroze and responded—but James was so close he didn't dare. Instead he just kissed her lightly again and let go of her, leaving her looking shocked and pale.

James changed the record to something more suitable for a party. Abby wondered whether he had noticed how Sam had kissed her—and whether he'd care even if he had. He seemed somehow to want to share her with Sam, as if his approval counted. A cold feeling crept down her spine. What if Sam let on that he *didn't* approve? She looked at him properly for the first time and noticed how quickly his hollow cheeks had filled out. He was wearing very fashionable baggy trousers in a dark blue wool fabric and a casual sweater over a cornflower blue and white striped shirt, open at the neck. James was in grey cords and a sports jacket. Before she could stop herself, Abby felt her heart sink with disappointment that he didn't look more dashing; that he hadn't shown a bit more imagination. Guiltily she crossed the room and began to study the records with him, shutting Sam out, making vacuous remarks—but nothing could shut out the overwhelming presence of their guest. He was there like a curse in her head, in her heart. There was a raw, animal sex appeal about him even when he was unwell. Like this, so dark and devastating, he was quite irresistible. Her lips stung where he had kissed her, and her shoulders burned where he had touched her... She closed her eyes and tried to control herself.

'Are you all right?' James's arm went around her as she swayed, and he led her to the sofa. 'You look incredibly pale, Abby. What's wrong?'

'Nothing, I'm fine,' she insisted, but she held on to his arm tightly. It was like a lucky charm, a talisman, a protection—though she didn't know what it was that had alarmed her so. So long as James was next to her, touching her, everything would be all right. 'I'm just tired,' she muttered as James continued to look down at her disbelievingly.

'I hope it's not a virus or something.' He ran his hand over her forehead and felt her pulse. 'My God, it's really racing! No wonder you keep flushing and then going white!'

'I'll get some water,' Sam said calmly.

Abby looked up and caught a brief shimmer of mischief in his dark, dark eyes. And then he seemed to take in the scene, James bending, concerned, at her side, holding her wrist and stroking the black velvet dress over her knees in an unconscious display of his concern, and he appeared to pull back. His eyes hooded themselves again and he was just as inscrutable as ever.

Before long the little flat was crowded with people. A knot of them were blocking the hallway and there were serious medical discussions going on in the study. Sam was there, with Jenny and a female houseman attired in a raspberry-coloured jersey dress that clung to her curves. Abby, collecting glasses and offering refills, watched their laughing faces turned up to their new hero; their smiles were fixed and dazzling, their lips parted. Even Jenny, who was normally so sensible, was talking with that extra animation that women develop when they come across a man they want.

Abby felt annoyed—it *had* to be annoyance, she reasoned as she edged past the houseman to collect an empty bottle from the bookcase.

'Of course, James has got it all worked out brilliantly. Joint replacement may not exactly be glamorous, not like the kind of thing *you've* been doing, Sam, but the NHS is never going to be able to cope with the demand. It's quick, it's easy, it's profitable and it's always going to be in fashion,' she was saying coyly. 'It's an option I'll be considering myself in a year or two.'

Sam twitched and looked over her head. 'I'd be very glad indeed if my kind of work went out of fashion.' His tone was dry and disapproving. 'When people stop shooting each other and the problems of drought and famine are resolved, *then* I'll start doing hip replacements.'

Hear, hear, Abby thought instantly— then stopped herself. What was she saying? James was a good, competent surgeon working most of the time in a Health Service hospital. He wasn't grasping or

98

looking for the main chance! And Sam Malone wasn't the saint he was making himself out to be. As she picked up the last paper plate James appeared in the doorway carrying a tray with glasses of wine on it. He stood chatting while people helped themselves and then suddenly, quite unexpectedly, Abby saw the tray just drop from his fingers. The crash of breaking glasses and the shriek of a nearby nurse whose dress was splashed with Beaujolais stopped all conversation dead.

James raised his eyes to the ceiling. 'I'm so clumsy! Sorry about this,' he apologised to the nurse. 'Abby'll help you sprinkle some salt on your dress and I'll clear up the mess in here. Abby?' He turned to her appealingly, like a naughty schoolboy.

'Are you all right, James?' Sam had left his harem and had squeezed his way across the room. The conversations had started again, and in the living-room someone had put on an old Rolling Stones tape. The strains of 'Brown Sugar' threatened to deafen everyone.

'I don't know what happened.' James tried to make it into a joke. 'I just seemed to lose control of my hands. I knew it was dropping, but I couldn't hold on to it.'

Sam was already picking up pieces of glass, and Abby restrained herself from kicking him. She resented his closeness to James, his constant intrusions. 'You've had too much to drink, that's the trouble,' he said now, laughingly. 'Abby, why don't you turn the tape down a bit and then get something to stop this wine staining the carpet?'

'Yes, of course, Dr Malone,' she said coolly. 'Have you any other orders for me, while you're down there?'

Sam looked up at her slowly, seeming to measure her as she stood in her demure black dress with its dropped waist and padded shoulders. He shook his head reprovingly. 'Temper, Abby, temper!'

Abby turned on her heel, stepped over the glass and, brushing past James who was still standing there in a state of shock, made her way to the kitchen. Her anger threatened to bubble over—yet she knew, at heart, that it was something irrational that she was feeling. Another of James's friends, seeing how surprised James was, might have done exactly the same thing. He might even, most of James's friends being doctors and on the bossy side, have given her orders as Sam had done. Would she have felt as furious with anyone else as she did now with Sam? As she returned to the scene of the accident with a bucket of water and a carton of salt she had to admit that she probably wouldn't. The room was empty except for a few stalwarts still arguing over current medical practice. James had taken Sam's place, picking up the bits, and Abby took her place beside him and began to mop up.

He pecked her on the cheek as she sprinkled salt over the stains. 'I thought I might make our announcement at midnight,' he whispered, and though she smiled at him and kissed him back, Abby couldn't control the shudder that seemed to creep down her spine...

'I know that most of you think you're here to celebrate the return of my good friend Sam to civilisation.' There were a few whistles and catcalls and shouts for Sam. James waited until they'd died down. 'But we're also here to celebrate something else.' He turned and pulled Abby forward, blinking and wondering why a smile wouldn't come to her face, in front of forty curious pairs of eyes. Jenny looked smugly knowing, and the truth had begun to dawn on several other people, too.

'Abby and I are going to be married. In fact we thought we'd get married as soon as possible, so that Sam can be best man!'

Cheers went up on all sides, and as if she was in a dream Abby felt herself being hugged and kissed—not by James but by Jenny and her other girl friends and then, it seemed, by nearly everyone else in the room. Disembodied voices were welcoming James to the married state; someone else was asking about the wedding. Had they planned it yet? Jokes about wedding rings and her skill as a cook echoed and reverberated in her head until she felt it would burst—and then, while she was being soundly hugged by one of James's pals, she looked over his shoulder and met Sam's stunned eyes.

He raised his eyebrows expressively, and she knew how the news had surprised him. But rather than look away he continued to gaze at her, and his eyes spelled nothing but disappointment. Not disappointment that he had lost any chance of seducing her, but disappointment *with* her, Abby thought wildly. 'I thought you could do better,' he seemed to be saying to her, and she cursed herself, because of course he was saying nothing of the sort. All these negative thoughts were coming from inside her own head. But *he'd* put them there! Before he'd arrived she'd never—she corrected herself—she'd rarely had a critical thought about James. And then he'd arrived, and he'd managed to throw everything into disarray. He'd sown seeds of doubt and poisoned their relationship, just as he'd infested their bed...

Someone else grabbed her and whirled her round, but Sam's eyes drew her back. He was still looking gravely at her. He was like one of those paintings whose eyes seem to follow you around a room, dogging you wherever you go. Abby felt the tears pricking the backs of her lids, but as soon as she found herself free of congratulating arms, she pulled herself up to her full height and glared back at him, tilting her chin as high as it would go and trying to recreate his own insolent look. Sam's eyes glinted back at her, meeting her challenge and reflecting her defiance. Then he raised his glass of apple juice to her and silently, alone among a crowd of dancing people, toasted her.

James swept her up now, and someone

dimmed the lights, and Abby tried to fight back the tears as she danced in the warm circle of James's arms. His chest was so broad she could lean against him with ease. He smoothed her hair, catching his fingers in it, playing with it. 'You can't believe how happy you've made me,' he murmured to her as they moved slowly around the floor, bumping gently into other couples.

The tears sprang up unbidden now, and she could hide them no longer. She pressed her face against his shirt, praying that this was all a nightmare and that she would wake up to find everything as it had once been. How could this have happened? She loved James, she did, she *did*... She tried to absorb herself into him, as if touching him would help her now. Only a few days ago his arm around her had been enough to ward off the threat of Sam Malone, but now it was too late. She stifled a sob, and for the first time James realised that she was crying.

'Hey, I know you're pleased too, but you don't have to get tearful!' he teased, smoothing her cheek. He felt in the pocket of his jacket and came out with a handkerchief and began to wipe her face. His touch was firm, rough almost. Abby straightened up.

'I'd like to go home. It's all been a bit too much for me.' She led him to the door. A few interested glances followed them, but most people were absorbed with each other. Out in the hall a group of non-dancing men were gathered at one end, while at the other some of the female wallflowers were talking about fashion and *Dynasty*. Fortunately no one had yet discovered that the bedroom was empty and she was able to draw him in and shut the door. 'You do understand, don't you, James?' she asked, beginning to search for her coat at the bottom of the pile. 'I just want a few hours to myself—to get used to being an almost-married woman.'

'Of course I understand.' He kissed her. 'That doesn't meant that I want you to go, though. You can stay here, Abby. Sam won't interfere. Didn't you see him drinking our health?'

'It's not him,' Abby lied, shaking her head. 'It's everyone. I'm tired and emotional and all I want to do is go home by myself.'

'I'll take you back,' James insisted. 'You can't walk home by yourself.'

'I *want* to. I need the fresh air, that's all.' Her head was beginning to thump protestingly. If she didn't get away soon, from the music, from the crowd, even from poor James, she'd go mad.

'And have you mugged? Come here.' He took her in his arms again and kissed her lingeringly. 'We'll walk home together and I'll kiss you goodnight on the doorstep, just like a fiancé should.'

'Please!' Her violent twist away from him surprised him. 'Don't make me angry, darling,' she heard herself say. 'I'm going to walk home along a main road with plenty of lights. It's only ten minutes—and if it makes you feel any better I'll ring you when I get there. But let me go alone. I just want time to...' She faltered. Time to...what? Time to decide she'd made a bad mistake? Time to decide whether she *could* go on with it?

James shrugged, obviously confused by her behaviour and quite unable to understand it. 'All right, if you insist.' He gave her a hopeless, lost kind of look, a look that he must have been using since he was a small boy, and always with the same result. 'Have I said anything, Abby? What have I done?'

106

'Nothing!' She tried to inject false brightness into it, and it sounded brittle.

'Are you beginning to regret that you said you'd marry me?' He looked like a spaniel that expected to be kicked, so reproachful and trusting that Abby felt new tears, this time of pity, rising to her eyes.

'No!' she cried, and whatever her thoughts of a moment ago, it really did come from the heart. 'I'm just beginning to realise the enormity of it all. Haven't you had a single twinge of nerves at the idea of living with me until death us do part?' She shook her head as if it might help to clear her muddled mind. 'It's a huge decision, James, and I can't take it lightly.'

'I can't think of anything I'd rather do than live with you for the next forty years,' he said quietly. 'We'll have our ups and downs, Abby, just like any other couple, but I want you to know that I'll never do anything to hurt you or let you down.' Abby could only hide her face in her hands. Every loving word was like a blow to her. He would never do anything to hurt her, so how could she even contemplate anything that would hurt him? How could she express her doubts, the sickening sense of dread that had filled her? She pecked him on the cheek and pulled on her coat, and he said nothing as she let herself out of the flat.

Outside, the air was crisp and so cold that it almost hurt to breathe. A thick frost crunched underfoot. Here, under a sky so clear that the stars were almost as bright as lightbulbs, she could put everything into perspective. She *did* love James. It was love that she felt when he looked at her with that adoring gaze. Maybe it wasn't a grand, passionate love she felt for him, but she did care very deeply.

The occasional car and even a night bus trundled up the hill as she made her way down towards the hospital and the flat she had been living in for the last few days. Sometimes she missed James, but her conscience pricked her for the easy way in which she'd returned to her old routine. She was so deep in thought that she wasn't aware of a tall dark figure following her up the path of the house. Only when she stopped to take the key from her bag did she realise that she wasn't alone. A hand snaked out and took the key-ring from her, inserting the key in the door. Her gasp of shock was muted as a strong arm pushed her inside the hall and the man followed behind her.

'It's all right, it's only me.' Sam's voice was muffled by the scarf he wore around his neck.

'What the hell are you doing, following me home like this?' Abby demanded indignantly.

'Be quiet, you'll wake the neighbours,' was all he would say, and he waited imperiously for her to open the front door of the flat.

'You're not coming in,' she said firmly. 'I've got nothing to say to you, particularly at this time of night.'

He shrugged his shoulders under the big overcoat. 'That's too bad, because I'm not going until I've said what I've got to say to you. I didn't want to wake the entire house up, but if you insist...'

'Just go, will you?' Abby opened the door and motioned him out. 'I'll call the police and tell them you followed me home if you don't!'

Sam gave her a look of disdain and ignored the empty threat. 'Five minutes, that's all it will take. Surely you can spare me that?'

'I wouldn't even spare you the time of day!' They stood across the hall from each other, a couple of yards apart, Sam with his hands in his pockets and a look on his face that told her he'd wait hours if need be. And he damn well *can* wait, Abby thought grimly. Whatever he had to say she could be sure it wasn't going to be pleasant, and she certainly wasn't going to allow him into her own home for the purpose of insulting her.

The impasse was broken by the sound of footsteps coming up the path and the unmistakably Welsh tones of Evan Williams, the pathologist who lived on the second floor, as he tried to find his key. Girlish giggles indicated that he was not alone. Abby watched Sam's eyebrows rise slightly and the hint of a smile lift the corners of his mouth. 'Someone else from the party,' he murmured quietly. 'I wonder what he'll think when he comes in and discovers James's brand new fiancée like this.' And before she could get away from him, Sam crossed the hall and took her in his arms. His mouth came down smoothly on her own, immediately silencing her protests, and despite her struggle he pinned her hands together behind her back so that

110

she could only kick against him. But even that backfired, as his only defence was to push her heavily against the wall so that every inch of her body was thrust against his. Her blood began to boil. How dare he? She hated him... But then his lips against her mouth, his free hand caressing the back of her neck as he held her fixed, began to strike that electric spark that set her alight, and she felt herself beginning to melt.

Something in him began to melt, too, Sam realised. At first he had just wanted to shock her, surprise her. He couldn't help himself. He'd never treated a woman this way before—never had to. Most of them fell into his arms without much encouragement whether he really wanted them or not. But Abby... He released his grip on her wrists, worried that he had hurt her. She still struggled in his arms, but only gently, and he felt her lips part under the insistence of his own. He twisted his fingers in her hair and bent to kiss her neck, and he couldn't stifle the groan of desire that rose in him.

Abby heard it, and though she knew in her head that she should be angry, that she should fight him off and shout

111

for help, her heart filled with something she had never felt when James kissed her. When she was with Sam her judgement seemed to go haywire. She either hated him so furiously that she couldn't face him or she found herself responding to him like this. She was drowning, and it was the most delicious sensation she had ever known...

The satisfying click of Evan's key in the lock roused her—but only so that she was precisely on cue to cast a guilty glance over Sam's shoulder to the Welshman's stunned face. 'Good evening,' he said, embarrassment making his ruddy face even more pink. An hour ago he had been present when his friend James Farris had announced his engagement to this girl. Now here she was in a passionate embrace with James's best friend. What was he supposed to think?

His girl-friend squeezed round the door too, only to stop short when she too took in the scene in front of her—Abby pink-faced and with Sam's arm firmly around her.

'Hello,' she said weakly, then Evan prodded her up the stairs. They disappeared silently, with only a single curious glance over the banisters, but Abby could hear them muttering between themselves on the top landing. A wave a nausea swept over her; real physical revulsion at the thought of what everyone was going to be saying tomorrow about her. Abby Andrews, the girl who was unfaithful to her fiancé on the night they got engaged. She felt her hands begin to shake, her head begin to throb. She must be going mad...

Sam took the keys from her and opened the door of the flat. It was dark and quiet. He switched on the light and she walked in.

'You've done what you wanted to do,' she said with more calmness than she felt. 'You'd better go now.'

'No,' he said firmly. 'Now I need to talk to you more than ever.'

CHAPTER FIVE

'Why are you going ahead with this charade? Why are you going to marry James?' Sam paced up and down the shared living-room of the flat. It was

cluttered with piles of records and books
and there were dirty plates and glasses
on the coffee table. Abby had made a
feeble attempt to clear them up, but he
had insisted that she sit on the saggy old
chintz sofa and listen to him. The clock
on the mantelpiece showed one-thirty in
the morning and she could hardly keep
her eyes open. It wasn't so much that she
was tired, just that she wanted to block
out the nightmare of the last few hours.
How could her life have fallen into such a
mess? Two weeks ago everything had been
as near perfect as she could ever hope it to
be. And now...

'I'm still waiting for an answer, Abby.'
Sam stood over her. 'Come on, try and
convince me that you're doing the right
thing.'

'I love James. I *do!*' Abby protested
as he turned away from her in disgust.
'I couldn't expect *you* to understand,'
she spat back. 'You wouldn't know the
meaning of the word!'

'No,' he agreed, coming back and
crouching at her feet. His eyes were
black and intent upon her, his body
ready to spring. 'I don't suppose I do
know what your kind of love is. But from

what I've seen, it's the kind of thing one normally feels for a pet or a child. You're confusing caring for someone with actually loving them, Abby. James runs after you like a puppy, he worships the ground you walk on—but I don't really think he knows much about you as a person.'

'Is that your diagnosis, Dr Malone?' Abby glared at him and wished with all her might that he didn't look so handsome. 'So you've framed me! Tomorrow my name will be mud at Highstead Hospital if Evan Williams lets on what he saw here tonight. And you don't care, do you? You don't care how much hurt you cause James, or me. Just so long as you can split us up, and all the while you justify yourself by saying that we're not suited and that you're only doing it for the best...' She paused for breath. 'How much do you know anyway? You've been back here ten days and you think you know what's best for us all—when in fact you're just full of jealousy and resentment that James is happy and has done well for himself, while you've got nothing to show for the last seven years.'

Her words struck home. Sam blinked and acknowledged that some of what she said was right. He had been motivated by sheer malice, the desire to stir up the water a little. But there was more to it than that. 'If everything is so perfect between you and James, then why did you burst into tears when he announced your engagement?'

Abby shook her head. 'I was overcome by excitement.' It sounded false to her ears.

'And what about this?' He leaned forward, across her, and pulled her face to him. And, just as he had done in the hallway, he kissed her again and again, holding her tightly until she stopped struggling and of her own accord kissed him back. It was madness. She *knew* in her heart, without a shadow of doubt, that it was madness. But there was simply nothing she could do to stop herself. When Sam touched her and murmured her name she had no choice but to respond. They could fight and disagree, she could say she hated him, even feel hate for him, but when he came to her like this it was as if they were made for each other. His hand cupped her breast and he buried his face in her hair, his lips teasing her earlobe, and she felt nothing but pure, animal longing for him—the same unthinking longing that he felt for her.

There could be a fire or an earthquake, but nothing could take him from this. He heard her sigh, and ran his hands down, over her hips, feeling her arch to him. And suddenly, with an almost superhuman effort, he stopped. A groan escaped from him, a groan that combined all his desire and disappointment and despair. He'd never wanted a woman as much as he'd wanted Abby. He'd gone months without female company when he was working and never felt like this. Even as a teenager, crazy for his first sexual experience, he'd never felt *anything* like this.

He raised himself from her and saw her flushed, surprised face. She tried to draw him back to her, but he resisted. He mustn't have her. The realisation hit him like a punch on the jaw. He might have toyed with the idea of seducing her; he might feel sure that she and James were badly suited; he might have lain awake at night in hospital wondering what it would be like to make love to her—but he couldn't have her.

Why he should suddenly develop this sense of honour, Sam didn't know. All he did know was that he couldn't betray either of them in this way. If Abby left James of her own accord that would be all right. But she wasn't going to, no matter what he said or did. And he couldn't entice her away, only to leave her in a few weeks' time with nothing. Grudgingly he admitted to himself that he cared too much for her to do that.

Abby watched these thoughts flicker in his eyes. She saw the pain and wanting in him, then the resolution as he stood up. It hurt her, though she could never have told him, to let him go. He had only to kiss her, touch her, murmur to her, and she could deny him nothing. She felt ashamed of herself for forgetting James so easily, but that couldn't still the beating of her heart. How could she allow herself to want a man like Sam, a man whom she'd never understand, not like James, who was so simple...

Sam took his coat from the chair where he'd left it. He was obviously aroused and still breathing hard. He wouldn't look at her as he put it on and pulled his scarf around his neck, but when he was ready and glanced at her, he saw that she was aware of his desire for her. A streak of anger shot through him. Damn it! Now she knew she had power over him, the power to make him want her. He cursed himself for getting carried away. 'Well,' he said cruelly, 'if you love James so much, maybe you'd like to explain to him what's just happened.'

Abby blushed and shook her head. Was that all it had been for? A way of proving to her that she wasn't as dedicated to James as she liked to think? 'I can't,' she said quietly. 'What are you going to tell James?' She buried her head in her hands and when she looked up at him there were tears in her eyes. 'If I could have just one wish, Sam, it would be that I'd never met you, that you'd never come here to ruin my life!'

'Don't bother wasting it on me. I'm not going to tell him anything—except that I left the party for some fresh air, bumped into and insisted on escorting you home. And I was just giving you a goodnight peck on the cheek when Evan, who'd had far too much to drink, came in and imagined that he'd caught us in a passionate embrace.' He gave her that wicked, twisted smile. 'After all, if I'd really wanted to make love to you I'd have brought you into the flat, wouldn't I, rather than seduce you in the hall for everyone to see.'

'Don't joke,' Abby warned him.

'I'm not joking. Your secret's safe with me.' He turned and let himself out, and a second later she heard the house door close and his footsteps crunching in the frost. She didn't know whether to believe him or not. Why would he try to ensure that James didn't believe Evan if he wanted to break them up? It didn't make sense—but then neither did her feelings. Slowly she rose and quietly checked the other rooms. One of her flatmates was on nights and the other obviously hadn't come home, so with relief she ran herself a bath and climbed in, hoping it would help her relax and sort out what was happening to her.

Half an hour later she had come up with only one possible solution—and it was an idea that seemed to undermine all her hopes for the future. Was it possible to be in love with two people at the same time? She did love James, no matter what Sam said; she cared for him deeply, couldn't imagine ever leaving him. That was love. And could she combine with that a physical desire for Sam so strong that it felt like love? Her toes curled in the water as she admitted it to herself, but it was true. She felt something for Sam that she'd never felt before. When he'd held her she'd wanted him so badly that nothing could have distracted her. She only had to think of him now, half naked as she'd taken off his clothes and put him to bed, to feel that spark ignite inside her and send all manner of thoughts through her head. This was the passion that was missing from her relationship with James...

She pulled her thoughts back to what she was actually going to do about it. She couldn't let Sam bully her out of the engagement, yet deep down she knew that some of what he had said was true. Even before he had arrived on the scene she had found herself wondering whether she and James were ideally suited. Somehow Sam's arrival had made her forget her doubts, but now they returned.

What if she were to call off the engagement? Then it would look like a victory for Sam. Even so, the flooding feeling of relief at the idea made her curse her stupidity in having allowed it all to get so out of hand. If only she'd trusted her instincts and said no to James, none of this would have happened.

The coldness of the bathwater reminded her that she had only a few hours in which to sleep. She'd promised James that she'd go and watch him play in the Highstead rugby team against St Angela's, and if she was going to have the courage to call their engagement off she'd need some sleep. It would go down, Abby thought as she slipped into bed, as one of the briefest engagements ever known—but better to be laughed at for a twelve-hour engagement than get married in error.

'Pass it! Pass it! Oh no!' The Highstead coach swore to himself, then turned to Abby, who was standing on the touchline trying to ignore the fact that James was playing very badly indeed today. 'How much did he have to drink last night?' he asked her sharply.

'Not much,' she replied. The doctors and surgeons took their rugger seriously, even though in James's case it would have been wise for him to give up. One serious injury and he'd be out of the operating theatre for weeks. Fortunately he was usually fast enough and tough enough to escape anything but a few bumps and bruises. This morning, though, he didn't seem to be able to do a thing right. He dropped the ball or passed it badly every time it came to him. Abby felt guilty. Maybe the way she'd behaved with him last night had upset him. And despite Sam's promise to smooth over anything Evan might say, she couldn't be sure that he was trustworthy.

Her attention turned to the game again. James had emerged from the scrum with the ball and taken off along the wing. He turned to pass the ball back to a forward, but before he had a chance to aim it, it seemed just to drop from his fingers. He watched in surprise as it rolled away into the path of an opponent, and then tripped over his own feet and fell down in the mud. 'He's coming off,' muttered the coach, trying to attract the referee's attention. 'It's the same with all of them. As soon as a woman appears on the scene they can hardly stand upright.' He cast her a disapproving glance.

James trotted off the field with his usual good grace. He knew he was playing badly, as his face indicated when he approached Abby. He was like a small boy at the school sports day who had let his mother down in a race, and she felt her usual caring urge to comfort him. 'I don't know what's wrong,' he frowned, pulling at his muddy fingers. 'I keep losing the feeling in my hands—my co-ordination's beginning to go.' He looked down at her and smiled. 'Sorry to drag you out here and then make a fool of myself. I obviously didn't get enough sleep last night—'

'I'd like a word with you, Farris, if you don't mind!' The coach glared at them both. 'If I'm not interrupting anything, that is.'

'Back in a minute,' spluttered James, and followed him, ready to hear the list of his crimes.

Abby turned back to watch the game. She didn't enjoy the sport, but since she'd met James she'd got to know quite a lot about it, and she knew every member of the Highstead team. Most of them had been to the party last night. Perhaps that was why they seemed to be playing particularly badly, she thought wryly.

'I can't see James. If you weren't here I'd have thought I'd come to the wrong place.' Sam's laconic voice interrupted her daydreams and made her start. Immediately she was jolted back to their scene last night—but in the clear light of a cold day things seemed different. It was difficult to imagine how they could both have been so swept away, though even under his layers of scarves and his big coat Sam still had an unsettling effect on her nerves.

'He's been taken off,' she replied, trying to keep her attention on the field.

'You mean I've climbed out of warm bed to come and watch him play and he's been taken off in the first twenty minutes?' He shook his head disbelievingly.

Abby looked at him mischievously. 'He was having a bit of difficulty catching the ball.'

'I see. Poor old James, he can't seem to hold on to anything at the moment.' Sam studied the legs of the player nearest them as if he had a professional interest in them.

'And what's that supposed to mean?' Abby demanded.

He shrugged with mock innocence. 'Exactly what I said. He's getting terribly clumsy. Milk bottles, glasses of wine, rugby balls—he can't hold on to any of them.'

'Why not add "girl-friend" to the list? That's what you'd like, isn't it? You'd like to see him drop me too.' She didn't feel angry with him, just drained. She knew what she had to do, now she had to find the right moment.

Sam grinned. 'If I didn't know better, I'd say you were getting paranoid, Abby.' He chucked her under the chin. To anyone watching it would have looked playful, but Abby knew that he was just asserting his authority over her, reminding her of what a single touch could do to her. 'I've got no intention of forcing you into anything,' he went on. 'I want both you and James as friends. But if your conscience tells you that you've got to...'

'Sam! Abby!' Jenny, pink-faced and panting, interrupted him.

'Hello, Jen! What are you doing here?' Abby called as her friend approached.

'I arranged to meet Sam here. We're going to see one of his old nursing friends—'

'Jenny expressed an interest in working with the kind of organisation I'm with,' Sam finished. 'I thought it might give her a better idea of what the life is actually like if she could talk to someone who's already been through it. Sarah Barnes, one of the nurses I met in Pakistan, has invited us to go over this afternoon.'

'Oh,' was all that Abby could say. It

was a bit like being plunged suddenly into shadow after bright sunlight. All along, she realised, she'd thought she'd had all of Sam's attention. The fact that he always seemed to be there, a brooding presence, had fooled her into imagining that everything he did revolved around her and James. To discover like this that he had been making his own arrangements that didn't include her came as something of a blow. How conceited she'd been to suppose that he had nothing better to do than meddle with her life. She looked across and registered how closely Jenny was standing to Sam, and how her face shone up at his. Another Malone camp follower.

'Too much to drink last night?' Sam called as James, dressed in cords and heavy jacket, joined them.

James raised his eyebrows heavenwards. 'I need a holiday, that's all. I'm getting tired and clumsy. Never mind,' he reached out and put his arm round Abby's shoulder, 'we'll be having a honeymoon before too long, won't we?'

Two pairs of questioning eyes focused on Abby's face and she hoped she hadn't blushed an incriminating red. Of all her acquaintances only two had ever voiced their doubts that marriage to James was a bad thing—and here they were, confronting her with looks that dared her to say something. 'We'll see,' she muttered noncommittally. 'Where does your friend live, the one who's going to give Jenny the run-down on nursing life in the bush?' she asked, changing the subject as quickly as she could.

'Near Cambridge. We'll have to go up by train. But we've got time for a coffee in Highstead before we set off.' Sam's voice was amiable enough, but Abby could hear the amusement in his throat.

'Good, I need something. And I can come back here when the match is over,' sighed James, looking back at the pitch and the mud-covered players as they began to walk away into the heart of the 'village'. Hundreds of years ago, when London had been a city bounded by walls, Highstead had been one of a number of remote hamlets dotted around it. It had developed a charm and character of its own, particuarly with its abundance of Georgian architecture, before being swallowed up into the mass of Greater London with the arrival of good roads and railways. These days it was only a ten-minute drive to central London. Two hundred years ago it had been at least half a day away by horse. Fortunately, although modern life had destroyed the countryside around, the central part of the village remained as it had been, tranquil and elegant. One of the old houses had been converted into a restaurant, and the four of them went in and ordered coffee and cakes.

'Surely you don't have to go up to Cambridge by train?' James protested as Jenny tried to work out a British Rail timetable. 'It'll take you hours!'

Abby wasn't listening. All she could think of was the fact that *she* would love to go up to Cambridge and find out what this Sarah person was like. Was she the tireless nurse who, with only Sam for help, had kept hundreds of orphans from starving? She sounded too good to be true, Abby thought cynically. If she was half as wonderful as Sam had made her out to be, she must be thoroughly obnoxious. Or maybe, just maybe, he had had a torrid affair with her in some desert hut... She pushed the salt and pepper grinders about on the table top and embroidered the scene. Sarah Barnes; it was a nice name. She'd be tall and elegant and ultra-cool. How would she have felt when Sam arrived to run the place? Abby took a covert glance at him across the table as he told a clever joke. His hair had grown slightly and was beginning to wave. His features were as strong and uncompromising as ever, with that firm chin and nose and those dark, twinkling eyes hidden beneath heavy lids. She swallowed and turned guiltily to James, who was saying something to her.

'You're not listening, are you!' he laughed. 'Not enough sleep last night, I suppose. Sam told me about your little problem with Evan.' He chuckled, and Sam cast a look that said *There, I told you so* in her direction. 'You'll drive Sam and Jenny up to Cambridge, won't you? It's only an hour and the traffic won't be too bad.'

'I don't know about that,' Abby retorted before she'd had time to think.

'The car's insured for me and you to drive, otherwise Sam could take it.' James waved the rail timetable at her. 'If they go by train they'll only have about twenty minutes to spend with Sam's friend when they get there.'

'Don't worry, Abby. The train will be fine, honestly,' Jenny chipped in, slightly too quickly to be thoroughly convincing. Abby saw her friend's eyes flash warningly before they settled on Sam again. Yes, Abby thought, Jenny wouldn't mind being locked in a railway carriage with Dr Malone for several hours. What better way to establish a relationship and really get to know each other?

'It's no problem,' she heard herself say. 'You're not coming with us, James?'

'I'm on call this afternoon,' he reminded them. 'In fact I ought to get back to the Sports Club now. The match will be finishing any minute and we've got to work out next week's training schedule. I'll just have one more cup of coffee before I go.' He passed his cup to Jenny and she filled it from the pot before handing it back to him. Abby wasn't watching—her eyes seemed automatically to move in Sam's direction—when there was a crash and Jenny let out a squawk.

'I've done it again!' wailed James, bending to pick the cup and saucer from the floor where they had fallen. Jenny was busy trying to mop up the pool of liquid on the table and an obliging waitress hurried along with a big cloth and soaked up the rest.

'This is getting beyond a joke,' Abby said crossly as she dabbed at the stains on James's trousers. 'What happened this time?'

Jenny threw the last of the wet napkins down on to her plate. 'I must have let go of the cup before James had it properly,' she explained. 'What's all the fuss about? Accidents do happen, you know!'

Abby smiled secretly to herself. Jenny was angry with her, and not because she'd been short-tempered with James. No, Jenny didn't want to be driven to Cambridge. 'Of course accidents can happen, Jen, but with James they seem to have become something of a habit.'

'Don't go on about it,' pleaded James. 'I don't know what's wrong. Everything's fine, then suddenly I find I've dropped things.'

Without a word, Sam leaned across the table and took James's hands. 'Do they feel cold?' he asked, and went on with a series of diagnostic questions. 'Got a penlight?' James offered him the silver penlight that he always carried with him and put back his head while Sam examined his eyes.

'Well, what's your diagnosis?' he asked playfully. But Abby could see that some of the fun had gone out of Sam's face. He studied James's eyes longer than he would have done if he was just mucking about, and when he sat down again, he gave him some simple tasks to do, including balancing knives on top of each other. James balanced them twice, but on each occasion toppled the pile by knocking them with his own hand. He turned questioningly to his friend.

Sam shrugged. 'Fresh air, no booze, plenty of sleep—that should sort you out. But maybe a few tests wouldn't be amiss. You might have some bug that's affecting your co-ordination...'

'Which reminds me that I've got to get back to the Sports Centre.' James jumped to his feet. 'I'll see you all this evening if I'm not out on a call. Oh, here are the car keys.' He pecked Abby on the cheek and fled, leaving the three of them silent and gloomy around the remains of their coffee.

Abby rummaged in her bag to find her purse and put the keys away. As she looked up she saw Sam's gaze following James down the road. A dark shadow seemed to pass across his face and then, when he saw her watching him, it vanished. 'Maybe we should be on our way too,' he suggested.

CHAPTER SIX

'Sam! Just look at you! I can't believe it!' Abby and Jenny stood back and surveyed Sarah Barnes's delighted greeting. Far from being cool and elegant and sophisticated, she was small, with short dark hair—and she was, at a rough guess, Abby estimated, about seven months pregnant. What was more, she seemed to be in her late thirties; at any rate, she was older than Sam. Jenny glanced quickly at her and they exchanged looks of mild surprise. Abby smiled to herself. So she hadn't been the only one who'd expected Sarah Barnes to be devastating! A twinge of guilt touched her as they entered the house, which was large and Edwardian and rather gracious. A woman who would give up some of the best years of her life to go and work in appalling conditions in a refugee camp would have to have vast resources of courage and determination and stamina. Why did she constantly seek to belittle such people with shallow judgements of them?

Sarah motioned them into a large sitting-room crammed with children's toys and exotic bits and pieces, probably brought back from Sarah's travels. Abby felt herself blush when he looked at her with that knowing twitch of his crooked mouth. It was as if he'd *known* of her suspicions about Sarah, as if he'd known all along that she'd automatically jump to the wrong conclusions. She felt ashamed, and not because she'd been so flippant about Sarah but because she suddenly realised what trials Sam must have been through too. No wonder he was so tough and ruthless!

'I'm sorry about the mess,' Sarah was apologising as she picked up her little son who was playing on the floor. 'Sam, here's your namesake, Sam Barnes. He's just turned two.' She held the child out to Sam, who took him gently, sitting him on one big hand while he bobbed him up and down a couple of times.

'There's no need to weigh him!' laughed Sarah. She turned to Abby and Jenny.

'Isn't that a typical reaction? Put a child in his arms and he automatically judges its weight!'

'I can hardly believe it.' Sam said quietly. 'You really shouldn't have named him after me, Sarah. What did your husband have to say about it?' Abby could tell, though, by the set of his lips and the light dancing delightedly in his eyes, that he was pleased. Little Sam sat contentedly in the crook of his arm, playing with his shirt buttons, quite relaxed and trusting. How many other children had he cradled like that? Children dying of starvation and disease? Had all of them felt safe and secure in the arms of this tall, dark, dangerous man?

'He didn't have much choice,' Sarah replied. 'Now, sit down all of you, and I'll go and get some tea.' She looked them over properly for the first time. 'Two prospective volunteers—that's good. Sam always had a way with the ladies.'

'Abby's only here as our chauffeur,' Sam butted in. 'She took one look at the railway timetable and volunteered to drive us up here,' he lied.

Abby bristled. 'Actually, I'm interested too.'

'Don't let James know!' laughed Jenny.

Sam looked up at her questioningly for a moment. 'Let me help you make the tea,' Jenny volunteered.

'I'd rather you didn't see the state of the kitchen, if you don't mind,' Sarah refused the offer of help. 'We had a dinner party last night and what with Sam and this,' she stroked her abdomen, 'and my husband having to be on duty at the hospital, I haven't had time to get things cleared away. I'll only be a minute.'

When she left them, Jenny went over to play with the baby. Abby sat down on the sofa, which was covered with a bright Indian dhurry, and watched them. She couldn't bring herself to kneel at Sam's side and watch him playing so tenderly with the child. She'd never, she thought, seen him being gentle and caring. He'd never shown any tenderness to *her*. Even when he had kissed her it had been with the force of lust, not love. It was almost as if he couldn't show her the softer side of his nature. Now she was seeing him as if for the first time, and she liked what she saw. How could she have ever doubted that he *did* have this side to him? This was what made so many people admire him and made him so good at his job.

She had brought out only the hardness and brutality of his nature. She bit her lip.

Sarah returned with the tea tray, and somehow her buoyant presence seemed to break down the uneasy atmosphere that had developed in the car on the way up and was still hanging over them. She got out thick photograph albums full of snaps of the various camps and compounds she had worked in. Some seemed pretty civilised; others left Jenny and Abby gaping with awe. Sam sat quietly in the background, occasionally adding an anecdote or a comment, but mainly watching. Little Sam lay asleep in his lap, and occasionally Abby saw him stroke the smooth forehead of the dozing child so softly that it made her want to cry. Why couldn't he touch her like that? The thought was instinctive; she flushed and turned back to Sarah.

'I think probably the worst,' she was saying, in answer to one of Jenny's questions, 'was Beirut. I was there with the Red Cross until 1982. We tried to work out of the main hospital, but it kept getting bombed. Conditions got so bad that we were doing major operations by torchlight. I can remember trying to assist at an operation to remove a bullet from someone's brain, holding a torch in one hand and passing instruments with the other, and all the while the shells kept coming over. Eventually one of them hit us and the ceiling came down. We saved the patient, though,' she added cheerfully.

Jenny pulled a face. 'I don't have much theatre experience,' she said. 'I don't know how much good I'd be in that kind of situation.'

'If you did apply for a posting abroad your experience would be taken into account. They wouldn't send someone with no theatre experience to a place where lots of theatre casualties were expected. Do you have paediatric experience?' Jenny nodded. So did Abby. 'Well, in that case they might find a use for you working with children. And you must both have spent time on a medical ward,' again they nodded, 'so in fact you could be placed without too much difficulty.' Sarah grinned. 'Anyway, all the experience in the world isn't necessarily useful when you get to a place with no facilities. You should have seen Sam when he first arrived! He'd got all these brilliant qualifications, but they didn't help him much. I'd never seen anyone so shell-shocked by it all!

After a couple of days I thought he was going to beg to be allowed to go back home. He didn't, though.' She reached over and pinched him mischievously, and he took her hand and squeezed it.

'If you hadn't been there I don't know what I would have done—I would certainly never have coped.' He smiled wryly. 'I was telling Abby only a week or two ago about the difference between what nurses are asked to do over here and the *real* nursing that people like you used to do.'

Abby remembered that afternoon, when he'd virtually pinned her to his hospital bed and told her how much he despised her and what she was doing at the Bentley. She couldn't forgive him for it, but maybe it was easier to understand how he felt now, having met Sarah and heard some of her hair-raising stories.

'You don't want to listen too much to what Dr Malone has to say, girls,' she told them firmly. 'He's one of those people who don't think you're doing anything good unless you're suffering. Just because you live for your work, Sam, it doesn't mean that everyone else has to. Arrogance was always your main fault.'

She said it laughingly but in such a

way that he couldn't deny it. 'Hear, hear,' added Abby. 'I'm glad I'm not the only one who thinks so.'

Sam aimed a playful kick at her, but she was aware that there was a blackness in his eyes; he wasn't amused. 'So what's my first step? I really do want to do this, Sarah,' Jenny asked.

'First of all, you've got to work out all the drawbacks in your own life and career, before you make any big decisions.' Sarah looked at them both keenly. 'You've got to be prepared to sign a contract for two years—or more, depending on the organisation you work for. And you won't make enough money to come back and settle down comfortably. Is that going to bother either of you? I was very lucky. I met Bob in Beirut and we decided to marry and come back here to have a family. Shortly after that his parents died and left us enough money to buy this house. But if things hadn't worked out like that I would have come back with no security, no house, no car—possibly without the chance of getting another job quickly.'

Jenny nodded. 'And if you'd spent all those years working over here you could have been in charge of a hospital by now.'

'Well, I could have been running a ward, at least. I'm not trying to put either of you off, I just want to point out that it will affect the whole of your life. You'll miss out on career opportunities and you'll lose what security you have at the moment. It's best to be aware of that now, rather than later. You both look fit and strong,' she smiled, 'but that's something else you've got to bear in mind. It's incredibly hard work, much harder than your present job. The hours are long and very often you can't get the kind of food you need to keep you healthy. If you know that you're the kind of person who gets ill or run down easily it's better not to think of going. You'll just be a liability to everyone else.'

'Like Stuart Miller,' Sam broke in. 'He was a terrific doctor but he didn't have the stamina for it. You remember him, don't you, Sarah?' He glanced at her keenly. 'He arrived with 'flu, which he promptly gave everyone else, and in the next four months he suffered everything that he possibly could. Dysentery, mumps, malaria...'

'Rather like you,' Abby couldn't help inserting. She gave him a frozen smile.

'Eventually we had to ship him back. He was more trouble than he was worth,' Sam concluded, ignoring her. 'Anyway, I don't know why Abby is so interested, because she's getting married in the next month or two.'

'It's not definite...' Abby tried to interject, but Sarah was already looking at her aghast.

'You can't possibly go off and leave your husband here! Is he thinking of joining too?'

'Well...'

'No, he is not!' Jenny said flatly. 'Honestly, Abby, the very idea of James setting off for the jungle is ridiculous! I've never met anyone more settled in their ways than him. And you know he wouldn't dream of letting you go.'

'We're not married *yet*, Jenny.' Abby tried to bite her lip and be silent, but she couldn't stop it slipping out. Jenny looked at her strangely and was quiet.

'I don't think I knew any married people who weren't working as a husband and wife team.' Sarah was thoughtful. 'How about you, Sam?'

All eyes were on Abby, and she could feel them boring into her. She felt like some kind of fraud, as if she was here under false pretences. Sarah must either think her an idiot or imagine that she was toying romantically with the idea without taking it seriously.

'I think it's really only for single people.' Sam's voice was quiet but strong. 'There are a lot of tensions involved in the work and I don't think they help to hold marriages together. You've got to be single-minded and answerable only to yourself, and you can't do that if you've got a husband or wife to worry about.'

'You'd better count me out, then, hadn't you?' It sounded rude, although she hadn't meant it to. How could Sarah or Jenny know how she felt? They hadn't had to put up with Sam's innuendoes and advances, his constantly blowing hot and cold. The other week he'd told her that the work she was doing at the Bentley was rubbish and that she really ought to be doing something more worthwhile, like working in the Third World. And now she was here learning about it he was virtually telling her to forget it. Last night he had urged her to call off her engagement with

James—in fact he'd persuaded her to do it. But now he was acting as if their marriage was a foregone conclusion. He was impossible to understand.

She got up and stood by the window, watching people crossing the green at the side of the house and walking down to the river. It was a tranquil scene; this was a tranquil house. She felt as if she had come in and disturbed it, like the spectre at the feast. Right at this moment she hated herself, hated Sam, hated the world for being so difficult to cope with.

Sarah went on with her advice to Jenny, giving her addresses and telephone numbers and suggesting other people that she might contact. Sam was silent, watching Abby's expressive back. Her shoulders were tense and she held her head defiantly high. He knew she was unhappy and he wished he could help her. But he knew that she was entangled in a situation that he could not solve. Every time he went to her, every time they spoke, he made things worse; and not because he wanted to, but because his confused feelings for her made him behave badly, irrationally. The child in his arms began to wake up and stare at him through half-closed, sleepy eyes. Then his little hand came up and touched the scar that ran from Sam's ear down to his jaw. Sam pressed the tiny fingers, sticky though they were, to his lips. He'd ruled out the possibility of his own children. They didn't figure in his future. This little Sam would have to be his representative in the next generation. Sadness seemed to overwhelm him at the thought and he closed his eyes against it for a second. Sometimes he wondered why he had decided to do what he had done with his life. Sometimes he felt so lost and full of despair with the world that he wondered how long he would be able to bear it. He needed someone to share it all with, both the joy and the pain, but because of what he had chosen to do he was destined to have to bear it all alone. He opened his eyes—and looked straight into Abby's, and they seemed to mirror exactly what he was feeling.

The journey back to London was almost silent. Jenny was very excited about the step she was about to take, but thoughtful too. Abby concentrated on the road as dusk fell and tried not to think of the man sitting beside her, lost in his own thoughts. It was dark by the time they got back to London and a penetrating drizzle had begun to fall. It was the fitting end, Abby thought, to a thoroughly miserable day. But the worst wasn't over yet. Now she had to go back to the flat and tell James that she couldn't marry him.

Quite when she had made up her mind to do so, she wasn't sure. Last night, in her bath, she had determined to put off the wedding, at least until Sam had returned to his posting and things were back to normal. But everything about today had struck home the fact that marrying James would be a mistake. The way she had begun to think and feel about him had changed. His presence was no longer enough to make her happy; in fact being with him seemed to unsettle her and make her unhappy at the moment. And listening to Sarah this afternoon had convinced her that what she really wanted to do was get out into the world and work hard for just a few years before settling down. She had got herself into a rut, and getting out of it would not be easy or pleasant, but she was going to do it.

Using the drizzle as an excuse, she dropped Jenny right at her front door so that she wouldn't come back to James's flat and get in the way. Now, Abby thought, she had to get rid of Sam for a few hours. 'Tell you what,' she said with feigned enthusiasm as Jenny disappeared into the house she shared with a variety of other hospital workers, 'why don't you go after her and ask her out for the evening? You could go and see a film or go out to dinner. Jenny would like that. I'm sure she's got lots of things she'd like to ask you if she could get you on your own.'

Sam looked at her quizzically, as if to say *What are you up to?*, then shook his head. 'No, I'm tired. I think I'll go back to the flat with you, have something to eat and go to bed. I've got a lot of thinking to do.'

Abby's heart fell. How could she have a heart-to-heart with James if Sam was in the next room? It was no use taking James back to *her* flat, either. Last night had been a fluke. Normally there was always someone in. And what she had to say to him tonight couldn't be said in a restaurant, however quiet or discreet. Driving up the hill towards Highstead village, she pulled the car into the kerb outside a pub. Sam would soon find out about it, so why not tell him now what she intended to do?

'I want you to do me a favour,' she said, turning to him. 'Would you go and have a drink in the pub, just for an hour or two?'

He looked at her as if she was mad. 'I'm on medication—I'm not drinking. And to be frank, Abby...'

'I don't want you to come and have a drink with *me!*' she interrupted. 'I want to have a good talk to James, and I can't do that if you're there. Please, Sam. I'm sorry to have to ask you, I know you're tired, but we need some privacy, just for a couple of hours. I need to get things sorted out.'

'What are you going to tell him?' It was difficult to make out his expression in the dark, but she thought for a moment that he looked anxious. 'I know it's nothing to do with me,' he added hastily, 'but if you're going to do anything stupid I'd like to know about it.'

'I'm not going to do anything stupid.' Abby sighed. 'If you really want to know, I'm going to take your advice and call off our engagement. It's the best thing to do. I want to think seriously about volunteering to work abroad, and I can't do that if I'm married to James.' There was a long

149

silence broken only by the cars coming up past them on the hill.

'Before you do anything, I want to tell you something,' said Sam. 'But it's too noisy here. Is there anywhere else we can go?'

'There's no need for you to say any more!' cried Abby, exasperated. 'You've said more than enough. I don't agree with half of it, but I'm convinced it would be for the best if James and I put a brake on things now, before they go too far. I need a breather to think things over, and I can't do that if he's steaming ahead with the idea that we're going to get married in six weeks' time.'

'There's something new that you've got to take into account.' Sam's voice was quietly commanding. 'Why not drive over to the Heath? We can sit in peace there, without pedestrians peering at us.'

'Oh, my God!' Abby looked out in the direction Sam was gesturing to and saw Evan Williams and his girl-friend walking by, waving jauntily. Their faces said it all. Perhaps the alcohol had dulled their memories of what they'd seen last night, but they hadn't made a mistake today. Abby quickly slipped the car into gear and they shot off up the hill as if the devil were after them. The Heath was only a five-minute drive away, and at night the car park by the ponds was deserted. She pulled up. If it weren't for the drizzle, a walk would have been appealing.

'So what's new?' she demanded, undoing her seatbelt so that she could face Sam properly.

'I don't think you should call off your engagement. Not yet, anyway.' He stared out through the windscreen.

'I don't believe this! You're trying to drive me mad!' Abby rubbed her eyes in disbelief. 'Last night you called it a charade and virtually told me not to go through with it. Now you tell me not to be hasty!'

Sam grabbed her by the shoulders and pulled her round to look at him as he spoke. 'Something has changed since last night. Something which alters everything.'

'*Nothing's* changed!' Abby flinched as she said it. If anything had changed it was *her*. Now she knew with certainty what she wanted. She wanted to investigate a new job. Her freedom, her chance to do something really useful with her life—she wasn't going to allow James or anyone to talk her out of that.

'Yes, it has, Abby.' Sam was serious. 'I think James is ill.'

'What?' Disappointment mixed with surprise dumbfounded her.

He shrugged helplessly. 'He's losing his co-ordination. I've only been in the flat with him for a couple of days, but he's been dropping things all over the place. It's not just his hands, he's stumbling too. You've seen it yourself—don't pretend it's not happening!' Abby cast her mind back. The image of the tray just dropping from James's fingers, his coffee this morning, the rugby match... It began to come together. The other evening they'd been out in the car and he'd suddenly fumbled the gear lever, couldn't get it to work. She'd had to tie his tie the other night because he couldn't pull the ends through the loop. And he'd tripped up and dropped the shopping on the stairs...

'What do you think it is?' she could barely ask. A cold cloak seemed to have wrapped itself around her.

'I don't know. He'll have to have a whole lot of tests before anyone can be sure.' He put his arm over the back of her seat, but she didn't want his form of comfort.

'You have an idea what's wrong, don't you?'

'You're not stupid, Abby. You know the symptoms as well as I do, even if you're too close to James to see it all clearly.' He ran his finger along the ridge of her ear. He was quite composed.

'I suppose it could be a brain tumour,' she said quietly. 'I've seen patients with that before. Some of them get very clumsy and unco-ordinated.'

'It could be, but I didn't see any indication in his eyes—though peering at his pupils in daylight in a café was hardly the best circumstances for an examination,' Sam replied. 'There are dozens of other possibilities, of course, some of them very minor. Colds make people clumsy.'

'He hasn't got a cold, and you know it.' Abby could hear her own voice as if it was coming from a great distance. The significance of the news was just beginning to sink in. 'How about multiple sclerosis? Or muscular dystrophy?'

'They're both possibilities.' Sam sighed. 'Unfortunately James is about the right age to start showing symptoms—'

'He's so fit! I can't believe it,' Abby protested. Then she realised how stupid that sounded. Diseases like MS didn't strike selectively.

'I'm sorry it's such a shock. I had to tell you,' he said quietly. 'It was just so obvious—because, I suppose, I haven't been living with him and watching it gradually creep up on him.'

'If it *is* something like MS he'll have to give up his job.' Abby's mind was beginning to look forward to the future. James wouldn't be able to operate if he couldn't control his hands. It would be a terrible blow to him.

'We don't know—so there's no point in immediately jumping to the worst conclusions.'

'He could end up in a wheelchair. Think how awful that would be for him!'

Sam's voice rose a note in exasperation. 'He'd be just as likely to go into remission! Abby, please don't start dwelling on things like that. It could be any of a dozen things wrong with him.'

She looked at him gravely. 'But what if it is, Sam? Can you think of anything worse that could happen to James? His work and his rugger gone—it would break his heart!' It was amazing how quickly feelings could change. Just a few minutes ago she had felt sure, one hundred per cent sure, that she would be doing the right thing by going back to the flat and telling James that it was all off. And now all her protective instincts towards him had come racing to the fore. How would he cope without her? What would he do? She remembered the slow disintegration of some of the MS sufferers she'd nursed on Men's Medical. Sometimes they went into remission and got better. Sometimes they were stable for years. But in a few the disease had progressed quickly and devastatingly, and there seemed to be nothing that anyone could do about it. Just a few months from now, if James was unlucky, and he could be in a wheelchair.

'I had to tell you before you went and said something to him. You understand that, don't you? I think it would be better if you said nothing for the time being, until we find out what's wrong with him. No one can make their minds up about anything until we know for certain. I know it's a mess, but there's nothing we can do.' Abby felt Sam lean across to her and stroke her cheek with the backs of his fingers. 'I feel as confused about the whole thing as you do.'

'If James *is* ill he'll need someone to look after him, won't he?' It wasn't the kind of question that really merited an answer. 'I'll have to do it, Sam. I couldn't bear to say no. He'll need someone more than ever now.'

'You're looking on the black side. We may find out in a couple of days' time that all this was melodramatic nonsense.' Sam tried to smile. 'Please, Abby, don't start jumping to conclusions. All I'm asking you to do is to keep quiet for a week or two. Forget what I ever said about you and James not being suited.'

'You've got a nerve, Sam!' she cried. 'Last night you were telling me I'd made a great mistake, and now you're telling me I haven't. What do you really think?'

He withdrew his arm from around her seat, shaking his head as if he really didn't know what to say. 'I think that sometimes in life things happen unexpectedly and change everything you believe. We all like to think we're in charge of our own lives, and then something like this happens and we realise that actually we're dependent on lots of other factors. Maybe if we'd both been free we could have done things differently, Abby. Perhaps I only said those

156

things to you last night because I didn't believe you'd really think about calling it off with James—I don't know!' He held out his hands helplessly. 'I'm bad at making decisions when it comes to relationships with people. I always have been a disaster.' He looked pained. 'I've hurt people in the past without thinking, people I'd not have hurt for the world if I hadn't been so impetuous. For example, when I first met you, I didn't hate you. I thought how beautiful you were, and how lucky James was to have you, and I suppose I resented it. He seemed to have it all. So I didn't stop to think, I was just as hurtful as I could be. I took it out on you without thinking. Can you begin to understand? I've missed so much. In the eyes of the world I'm a failure, really. I don't have a house and a car and a beautiful girl-friend, and they're what count in this day and age. And there was James, with you and all the trimmings.'

'I thought that kind of thing didn't matter to you,' Abby said quietly, stunned at his confession.

'They don't. The last thing I'd want right now would be a semi-detached and all the responsibilities that go with it.

157

Maybe one day, when I get to be too old to be useful, I can come back. I'll never starve, anyway.' He sighed. 'It's just taken this news about James to put things into perspective, that's all.'

Abby thought hard. At last she began to understand, and at last she began to realise what she had to do. Maybe part of her loved Sam's romantic image, but what he'd just said made sense. And right now it was James who mattered most. As Sam said, sometimes you just had to go along with things; you couldn't always dictate the terms of your own life. 'I'm not going to say anything to James. I'll stick with him for as long as he needs me,' she said gently, snapping her seatbelt in place.

'Good,' came the calm voice beside her. 'I hoped that was what you'd say.'

James wasn't in when they arrived at the flat. He must, they presumed, be out on a call. 'He usually leaves me a note,' said Abby, searching the kitchen for one. 'Maybe it was an emergency.' She made supper for them and took it through to the sitting-room and they ate it off trays while watching a black and white film. Silence hung heavily in the air between them. There was really nothing more to be said until James came back and they were able to talk to him. Sam's last words rang in Abby's ears as she picked at her lasagne. What had he meant by saying that he'd hoped she'd insist on sticking with James through thick and thin? Where were his protestations of last night? She watched him covertly as he ate and saw the tiredness and pain reflected on his face. Maybe, just maybe, he was only human too and got carried away at times.

Her thoughts were interrupted by the telephone and she went to answer it. It was Ian Harvey from Men's Medical. 'You've come back at last,' he said gravely. 'We've got a bit of a problem, Abby. James collapsed at the Sports Club this lunch time and we've admitted him for tests. He'd like to talk to you, and so would I. Can you come over?'

Abby felt her stomach lurch. 'Is he all right, Ian?'

There was a telling pause. 'He seems to be, yes. We've done a scan and it's fine. It's probably nothing to worry about, but I'd just like a chat with you.'

'I'm on my way.'

She put the phone down and turned round. Sam was standing in the doorway,

159

dark and brooding. 'I think I got the gist of it. Do you want me to come with you?' he asked.

'No.' Although shaken, Abby felt cool and in control. She was not going to have him steamroller everyone again. 'Believe it or not, it's nothing to do with you. It's just me and James.'

Sam watched her leave, and something compelled him to peer out of the study window and watch her walk down the road towards the car, too. Bitterness rose in his throat and threatened to choke him as he admired the firmness of her step and the way her hair swung, glinting in the lamplight, as she moved. If he hadn't had his suspicions about James this morning, the engagement might have been over by now. But something in him, some old and surprisingly deep loyalty to James had made him spill it all out tonight, his fears for James's health. And he'd known that Abby wasn't the sort of girl to walk out on a sick man. It was almost as if he had given her back to James. Last night she could have been his, and today he had lost her.

He looked at his few possessions scattered around the small room. It would

take ten minutes to pack, and then he
would be free to go anywhere he wanted,
anywhere in the world. He could go and
stay with his sister in Ireland, maybe, or
his parents in the States. Or he could take
a plane to Nairobi and get straight back
to work. He began to pack, putting away
the books, folding the clothes, the few vital
bits and pieces he needed. The grey kitbag
was soon full. All he had to do was leave
a note, put on his hat and coat and he
could be off.

From the kitchen wall he took the
notepad and the red pen. *Dear Abby*,
he wrote. It sounded wrong. *Abby, I've
decided to leave.* It was the truth, maybe,
but it didn't tell her why and it was brutal.
He tore it off and started again. *Darling
Abby, I've decided not to hang around and
mess up your life any longer...* He stared
at it and wondered why it sounded so
melodramatic, before tearing it up too.
Was leaving the right word? Maybe he
was just running out on her at a time
when she needed him. She didn't know
that she needed him, perhaps, but she did.
And if James's illness was as serious as he
half-suspected that it was, she would need
him all the more. Instinct told him to get

out now, before he became too involved, but something stronger held him back.

Slowly he returned to the study and began to unpack.

CHAPTER SEVEN

'How's James?' asked Jenny stifling a yawn. It was a quarter to eight in the morning and she and Abby had just arrived to take over from the night shift. They had gone over the details of things that had happened in their absence and now Carol, as senior staff nurse, was organising a schedule for the morning.

'No change,' Abby murmured as she read through the overnight reports on her patients. 'He's got them totally confused. The more tests they run, the more uncertain they are...' She bit her lip. James had been in hospital for more than a week now. He'd been over to the consultant neurologist at St Brendan's and had had the attention of some of the most eminent doctors in London—yet still no one could make a diagnosis. And

162

meanwhile James was getting fractious. His enforced confinement had meant that the patients on his list had had to go to another firm. His fellow medics were polite but already distancing themselves from him, as if he had leprosy. No one would admit it, but as far as many of them were concerned James's days as a surgeon were numbered—because the general consensus seemed to be that he was suffering from some form of muscular disease. If it wasn't multiple sclerosis, Ian Harvey had as good as told her, it was something similar.

Jenny looked at her friend and saw the dark shadows of strain and tiredness under her eyes. She patted her gently on the shoulder. 'They'll find out soon enough. If it's got all the doctors flummoxed it's bound to be something so simple that they're overlooking it. That's what happens in most of these cases.' Abby tried to smile cheerfully. 'Do you remember Mrs Dodd? In here twice with asthma, and everybody at their wits' ends, and then they discover that she's allergic to the pills they're giving her for her diverticulitis. Six weeks it took them to work it out, and after that she was as right as rain.'

'They'd better find out soon,' sighed

Abby. 'He's getting very bored. I would have thought that Sam could visit him every day, but he seems to have found himself something better to do.' She stopped herself from saying anything she'd regret later. After all, Jenny was a fan of Sam's and she'd defend him.

Jenny grinned enigmatically and went pink. 'I've seen him a couple of times, so maybe you should be blaming *me* for keeping him busy.'

At that moment Carol looked up and began to announce who would be doing what today, and Jenny's words were drowned. 'Mrs Ubaldo and Mr Dunbar were discharged as planned yesterday afternoon, so we've now got two empty beds, and neither is scheduled to be filled until next week. That means that Emma's down to one patient, so I'd like her to special Mr Ollard-Gore, who's still very poorly. We'll need to watch him carefully. Abby, I've asked Sister to come down and have a look at him and at Miss Kendall and Mrs Carrington as soon as possible. We'll both go round with her. She'll do a second round at eleven, if that's okay for your patients, Jenny?'

'The physio's due round then for Miss

Kendall's percussion, but otherwise that's fine,' Jenny nodded.

'Good.' Carol pencilled a note on her list. 'Two things to keep an eye on, please. The first is Mr Petry's drip, which has been playing up all night, and the second is Mr Drinkwater's BP. Hourlies for him, please, Abby. In fact he's due about now,' she finished, consulting her watch.

'I'm on my way!' Abby got up and went to collect the sphyg and stethoscope from the prep room. With so few patients to look after, most were checked at least hourly, anyway. In fact some of them were checked so often that they began to resent the constant intrusions and interruptions. Mr Drinkwater had had a prostectomy. He was recovering well and had given them no cause for concern except for his erratic and sometimes alarming blood pressure.

It was worryingly high again now, Abby thought as she checked the sphyg reading in case she'd made a mistake. No, she hadn't. She settled him comfortably before using the automatic switches at the bottom of the bed to raise his feet and legs slightly above his head.

'Don't worry,' she explained as he protested. 'It'll make you feel better. I'm going to ask Sister to come and visit you in a minute, so stay where you are, please.'

She made her way quickly back to the staff room. In a normal hospital there would have been no problems with a case like this. Sister would have been on the ward and immediately available. And if drugs or treatment were required it wouldn't take long for a doctor to be located so that he could make a prescription or examination. But here there was only one resident doctor and he was usually busy. What was more, he didn't like to interfere with other people's patients. If a surgeon or private specialist was supervising a patient they often objected very strongly to another medic prescribing extra drugs. They expected to be called out so that they could make the decision themselves—even if it meant the poor patient waiting for hours until they could be located!

When she got to the staff room Abby found that Sister was already in with Mr Ollard-Gore, a cerebral haemorrhage patient who wasn't really expected to live. She walked swiftly to Mr Ollard-Gore's room. Sister and Emma were turning him.

'Ah, Nurse, come and give a hand, will

you? And when you've done that, arrange for Mr Wynyard to visit his patient,' Sister Bradshaw said. She was an attractive woman with a naturally authoritative air about her. Secretly Abby thought that she rather enjoyed her position of power at this glamorous hospital. She seemed to revel in her contact with the patients' relatives and friends—in fact she positively sparkled in the wealthy and sophisticated atmosphere that the Bentley cultivated.

'Certainly, Sister, but actually I came to consult you about Mr Drinkwater, the prostectomy. His BP's high—' she quoted her most recent reading '—and he's experiencing some breathing difficulty. Would you come and look at him, please.' Abby stood her ground as Sister pulled a displeased face and consulted her watch.

'This is too bad! I've got a cardiac case upstairs causing problems and Mr Ollard-Gore here. Now Mr Drinkwater! Come on, then, let's have a look at him.'

Emma raised her eyebrows in a look of harassment as they left the room, and Abby smiled inwardly. Perhaps now she was beginning to learn that life here could be just as difficult as in any hospital!

Back in Mr Drinkwater's room Sister

repeated the routine checks for herself. She picked up the chart at the end of the bed and studied it, before bidding Mr Drinkwater farewell and walking a few yards down the corridor before turning to Abby. 'Right, call up his consultant and ask him to come as soon as possible. Meanwhile I want you to check him every fifteen minutes.' She checked her watch again. 'I wanted to check Miss Kendall's dressings before her specialist visits this morning, but I can see I'm not going to have time. Would you and Nurse Hall take a look, please, and make sure that everything's all right. I've got a funny feeling there's a slight infection there, and it will look better if we can inform *him* of the fact before he spots it for himself.' And with that she was off down the corridor.

Abby did as she had been told, arranging for the various consultants to make their visit. Fortunately breakfasts were supervised by service staff, and so was the cleaning of the rooms, but even so it was a hectic morning. She assisted Carol in the drugs round and answered calls from relatives when Carol was busy. Together she and Jenny bathed two of their patients and washed the others. These duties were usually performed by the night staff in a hospital, but the Bentley didn't have the same kind of routine for its patients. After all, they were paying a small fortune each day they were there: it would have added gross insult to injury to wake them at six in the morning.

It was gone ten when they finally got around to Miss Kendall. She had had a breast augmentation three days previously and was lying rather uncomfortably propped up on her pillows, watching a video. 'What is it this time?' she asked flatly as they came in with the trolley, which supported a sterile tray and all the paraphernalia required for the aseptic dressing procedure. 'I've had a bath, if you could call it that, and I've had the physiotherapist in to arrange an appointment. Though what I need *that* for I can't think. Oh God,' she complained as she realised what they were going to do, 'have I got to take my nightdress off again?'

Jenny tactfully explained what was required, and very swiftly she and Abby removed the soiled dressings and swabbed down the skin. It was black and blue and looked as if it would never heal—but it would, Abby knew from experience, and probably no one would ever realise that Miss Kendall's bust was fifty percent silicone. 'Can I see?' the patient asked, forgetting her boredom.

'Not quite yet.' Jenny tried to make a joke of it. 'Your surgeon will unveil it to you in good time, and we wouldn't want to steal his thunder. Are you still very sore?' she asked, trying to distract her attention while Abby gently checked for any sign of infection. There was none as far as she could see. In fact it was all very clean and tidy apart from some dried blood here and there.

'I'm in absolute purgatory,' Miss Kendall snapped, 'and it's mostly due to all this prodding and poking! I just hope it's worth it, that's all. You wouldn't believe how much this has cost me!'

Jenny winked at her colleague as they scrubbed up and prepared to apply the new dressing. They could both guess how much it had cost, and they both privately thought it was a waste of money—though of course, no one at the Bentley ever mentioned such a thing.

Emma was in the staff room when Abby returned. 'Mr Ollard-Gore's been moved downstairs. They've got a spare agency nurse to special him,' she said quickly, almost as if she were afraid Abby was going to accuse her of shirking.

'Poor old thing,' was all Abby said. They'd got into the habit of calling Mr Ollard-Gore by the more amusing name of Mr Bollard-Bore because he was such a bossy patient—something very high up in the Civil Service, they'd heard through visitors. Despite his sharp tongue, it wasn't pleasant seeing him shunted off downstairs to another ward. 'What about Mr Drinkwater's consultant? Has he been in yet?'

Emma looked vague for a moment. 'Yes, I saw someone going in there earlier. With Sister.'

That at least, made Abby feel a bit happier. She hated the thought of a patient having to wait hours for attention. She picked up Mr Drinkwater's notes. There was no signature indicating a visit and no change in medication, which was very odd. She was just about to say something more when Carol breezed in.

'Abby, you take early lunch. Jenny's taking second, Emma, you can take one o'clock and I'll take one-thirty. You'd better get off, Abby,' she said gruffly, with a meaningful glance at the clock.

'One of you will have to do the obs for Mr Drinkwater,' Abby pointed out as she went to take her handbag from the locker in which it was kept. 'And I think we should check whether his consultant has been in or not. Emma thought she saw him...'

'We'll cope.' When she was busy and tired, Carol could be very abrupt, and she was obviously in a mood now. Abby decided that discretion was the better part of valour and left. If between them Sister and the senior staff nurse couldn't keep track of who was doing what then there was little hope for the ward.

The Bentley's staff canteen wasn't quite as splendid as the rest of the building. In fact it was fairly obvious that it had been added on as an afterthought. In the shadowy semi-basement of the building it was almost as gloomy as the Highstead canteen. The food was better, though. Not a patch on the kind of thing the patients ate, but freshly cooked all the same. Abby selected some chicken pie and vegetables and sat down at an empty table. There weren't many people about, and very few of them knew each other anyway. It was so unlike Highstead, where you always met friends at lunch and the meal became a real break. Here, she thought sourly, she might as well be in a station buffet.

Thoughts of James insisted on crawling into her head as she ate, no matter how much she tried to block them out. For days now she had been living in something close to a state of shock. At least, that was what it felt like. She didn't know what to do or think; all she could do was try to live with this dreadful, nagging knowledge that she could do nothing about. She finished her meal and picked up her coffee cup, cradling it in her hands.

What was most frightening of all was the horror that filled her at the thought of her future with James. His illness should, she knew, have brought them together. But instead she felt quite empty at the idea of going through life with him in a wheelchair, slowly degenerating and losing control. This in turn made her feel angry with herself, and with James for making her angry. She'd found herself talking sharply to him last night, and had been even more upset by the look of bewilderment on his face. After all, he'd seen how tender she could be with her other patients—so why was she being so tough on him?

Abby pressed the still warm cup to her cheek. She closed her eyes and tried to imagine how it would be if everything turned out all right; if they suddenly discovered James's problem was caused by trapped nerves, or a rare virus, or even an operable tumour... Despite the blast of the central heating and the warmth generated by the kitchens, a cold shiver passed down her spine. The image of James fit and well and ready to marry her didn't make her feel any better. That horrible empty feeling still remained. There was only one glimmer of light and hope in her dark world, and he was forbidden to her now. Whatever happened, Sam was out of reach.

With the news of James's illness, he had changed. He was out whenever she had gone to the flat to use the washing machine or to pick something up for James, and this morning Jenny had confirmed that he'd been out with her. It was obvious what had happened. Until the other week it had all been a game. The idea of luring James's girl-friend, of making a few waves on the calm pond, had been harmless fun. Now things were different. James's illness had changed it all and made it much more serious, and Sam had withdrawn. He didn't want to get involved now. He didn't even want to visit his old pal in hospital, and that was what hurt most of all, even more than his apparent rejection of *her*. She blinked away a tear and told herself not to be so self-pitying. A man who could be so self-centred was not worth crying over.

Leaving the canteen, she went off to the cloakroom, let her hair down and brushed it out before twisting it up again and pinning her hat on top. The bluish fluorescent light seemed to drain her of what little colour she had, making her look washed-out. Abby stared at her image in disgust and tried to rectify the worst of it with a little light blusher and a smudge of pink lipstick. Heavy make-up was frowned upon here, as in all hospitals, but the Bentley liked the nurses to make the most of themselves. Feeling marginally better, she made her way up to the ward.

As she came out of the lift, a tall figure emerged from the waiting room at the end of the corridor. 'Sam!' Her delighted cry had slipped out before she had a chance to check it. 'What are you doing here?'

He looked at her incredulously—at the old-fashioned uniform and her neat curves outlined by the broad elastic belt round her waist. 'I thought for a moment I'd died and gone to heaven,' he joked, coming over to her and pecking her on the cheek as if she were his elderly aunt. There was no passion in it; they could have been brother and sister for all anyone watching would have known. Abby felt her initial reaction die in her throat.

Sam fought to remain cool and casual. After all, he'd decided that he wouldn't touch her or get too near her again, hadn't he? It was simpler all round if they kept out of each other's way, avoiding all temptation. That way Abby would soon realise that her job was to support James, stay by his side in sickness and in health, for better, for worse. If he hadn't come along, the pair of them would still have been living together, still as in love as when he'd erupted on to the scene. If James had gone down ill three months ago there would have been no doubt about Abby sticking with him. Now...

He swallowed. She looked wonderful, even if the uniform was like something he'd only seen in a museum. All he

176

wanted to do was reach out and touch her; instead he gave a deliberately casual shrug. 'I was looking for Jenny, actually. Is she around?'

'I expect so.' Abby struggled to stop the disappointment from showing. She could feel the corners of her mouth drooping by the second, pulling into a miserable pout, and there seemed to be nothing she could do to prevent it. So he'd come for Jenny. For a moment, when she'd walked out of the lift, she'd imagined he'd come to see *her*. She felt her anger begin to rise. How dare he behave like this, as if there had never been anything at all between them? As if he'd never kissed her and urged her not to marry James? How hypocritical could a man be?'

Sam saw the defiant angle of her chin and guessed what she was feeling. He longed to put her right, but he resisted the desire to tell her that he suspected that he'd fallen in love with her. Hell, it wouldn't last—it never did. And right now James needed her more than any other man.

'You shouldn't be here, you know that?' Abby asked coldly as they turned into the staff area.

'I've never been one for worrying about rules,' was all he said. He looked about him with a mixture of awe and contempt for the surroundings. 'This place is just like a five-star hotel! How on earth do you get any work done with all these acres of corridors? And what happens if someone bleeds on the floor?'

'The carpets are Scotchguarded. They don't stain,' she replied flippantly. 'To be honest, I don't care what you think.' They went into the staff room, but Jenny wasn't there. 'You can't stay. Sister'll have a fit if she finds you here. Give me your message and I'll pass it on to Jen. And next time try phoning instead of just walking in.' She didn't look him in the face; in fact she couldn't bear to, so scared was she of seeing indifference in his eyes. If he would just take her in his arms, hold her, tell her everything was going to be all right, she might be able to bear it. But this pretence that there was nothing wrong, nothing going on... It made her feel as if she was being torn to pieces.

'Pass what on to me?' Jenny came pattering in, her arms laden with video tapes in their boxes. 'Sam!' she squealed, dumping her load on the table. 'What are you doing here?' Their kiss, Abby observed, was distinctly warmer than one between casual acquaintances. She thought her heart had reached rock bottom, but she felt it drop even further.

'Just look at the pair of you!' Sam said wonderingly. 'I wonder how much it costs just to keep you in those uniforms.' Abby turned away to fill the kettle. If she could have disappeared right now into dark oblivion she would have been happy. 'Actually, I came to tell you that I'm going to have to call off dinner this evening. I've got another duty to do.'

'I don't suppose that would mean that you intend to visit James?' Abby asked sarcastically. 'You seem to have been neglecting your duties *there*.'

'I can't go and see James—not tonight.' Sam looked guilty. 'I'll go and see him this afternoon, Abby, if you think I should. I just don't want to get between you. This must be a very tough time for you both...'

Abby turned her most withering gaze on him. 'How very considerate of you!' There was an uncomfortable silence. Sam broke it by reaching across the table and picking up one of the video cassettes. It featured a lurid thriller.

'What are these for?' he asked quietly.

'One of my patients.' Jenny looked at him with her head on one side. 'Nothing but the best at the Bentley, you know! And I *know* what you think, Sam. You're just about to launch into a tirade against this place and the uniforms and the carpets and trained nurses running errands with videos...'

'I'm obviously getting predictable.' He tried to smile, but Abby could see that he was really angry. His lips tightened in a line, not in the wonderful crooked expression that lit his face when he was genuinely pleased.

'You said it,' she nodded airily.

Jenny took a step backwards, exasperated with the pair of them. 'Abby, you know as well as I do that videos are normally dealt with by the service staff and not by nurses. What's got into you two? You're like a pair of dogs who've been in a scrap!'

As she finished the last word Mr Drinkwater's light went on and the buzzer sounded as he pressed the call button. Without stopping or even bothering to explain to Sam where she was going, Abby went to answer it. No matter how bad he had felt before, Mr Drinkwater hadn't used his call button, and she anticipated what had happened to him even before she entered the room. He was lying sprawled on the bed, his face white, his hands clenched. He had had the heart attack that had been indicated by his high blood pressure. Abby went to take the emergency bell from his fingers and pressed it three times in the prearranged signal. Then she heaved him into the centre of the bed and felt for the carotid pulse in his neck. Although she knew the routine and had coped with many an infarction in the past, she couldn't stop her fingers from trembling. Consequently she was still trying to find a vital sign of life when Jenny arrived—and right on her heels, Sam.

'He's arrested,' she informed them tersely. 'We'll need the trolley from upstairs with all the gear. Call up a doctor, any doctor.'

'There's no need.' Sam had already pulled off his overcoat. 'Fetch the adrenalin first, then go for the equipment. Is there a Sister on the ward?'

'She'll be at lunch. What are you doing?' Abby cried as Sam dragged the patient from the bed and laid him out on the floor. Jenny fled.

'No bed board. It'll be far easier to give heart massage on the floor—those interior sprung mattresses absorb the blows.' He ran a practised hand down Mr Drinkwater's neck. 'There's a stethoscope in my inside coat pocket. Get it!'

Abby felt mesmerised. It wasn't that she didn't know what to do, just that Sam seemed to have taken over the situation so completely that she didn't have to think for herself. Once or twice she'd seriously wondered what kind of a doctor he'd be. Now, faced with this crisis, she could appreciate his toughness and singleminded attitude. Fortunately she found the stethoscope quickly and handed it to him. If she'd taken long she knew full well what he'd have to say to her.

'He's been out about a minute and a half,' she murmured as she watched Sam carry out a brisk sounding of the patient's chest.

'Good,' muttered Sam, pulling back the inert body's pyjama jacket. 'I'll start trying to resuscitate him. You keep a note of the time.' He placed both hands, one on top of the other, just between the breastbone and gave a sharp blow. Abby imagined she could hear the ribs groaning under the strain. In training they'd been told it was far better to crack a rib or two than not use the technique firmly enough; Sam's wiry strength was quite capable of doing some damage.

'Here you are!' Jenny came tearing in with a kidney dish and syringe. 'I had to find Carol for the keys to the medicine cupboard, that's why it took so long. She's gone to get Sister.'

'Try a hundred ml,' growled Sam, his hands pumping vainly at the pale ribcage. Abby inserted the syringe into the rubber cap of the bottle and drew up the liquid. Pulling it out of the phial again, she tapped it, an automatic reaction to get rid of any air bubble trapped inside and, holding it up, released a little through the hypodermic needle. Then she lifted the inert arm nearest her, pressed hard to find the blue vein, and emptied the adrenalin into it.

Jenny had disappeared again in search of an oxygen cylinder and mask when Abby looked up. 'I can't believe it,' Sam puffed. 'All this money and yet you don't have a cardiac trolley on every floor! What about the house doctor!'

'There's just one, but he's never available

when he's needed. Everyone else has their own consultant.' She placed the stethoscope to the pulse point and thought she heard something. 'Keep going, you're there!' she cried. 'The adrenalin's done the trick.'

Sam glanced darkly at her. 'Sheer brute force, that's what's done it. Take over for a second, will you?' Abby moved around the patient and, placing her hands where Sam's had been a moment ago, took up the rhythmic pumping. Sam tilted Mr Drinkwater's head back, opened his mouth and peered down his throat. Without any sign of distaste he removed the plastic dentures and then, holding the patient's nose, gave him the kiss of life. Abby studied the back of Sam's dark neck and wondered why, in the midst of all this chaos, she felt so calm. Here they were in a life-and-death situation, yet it all felt as if it was under control. She didn't for a moment doubt Sam's ability to revive Mr Drinkwater; she had total confidence in him. If it had been James in his place, she'd have been worrying, anxious on his behalf, but not with Sam. There was something quite different about him.

Suddenly Mr Drinkwater gave a rasping

intake of breath and began to breathe again of his own accord. She stopped her cardiac massage and Sam sat up, wiping his mouth with the back of one hand as he reached for the stethoscope that hung round his neck. A fine film of sweat shone across his brow. 'How long?' he asked briskly.

Abby checked the watch that dangled from her breast pocket. Designed especially for nurses, its face was upside down so that when he lifted it towards her she could read it properly. 'Three minutes eighteen seconds. He should be fine.' There was a critical time limit when it came to cases such as these. If the oxygen supply to the brain wasn't maintained then permanent damage could be done. It was established procedure to keep a careful check on the length of time for which a patient stopped breathing. 'Phew!' Something in her wanted to make light of the situation. 'It's a good job you were here—that could have been a close shave.'

Sam glowered at her. 'He would have been dead, and you know it.' At that moment, the sound of running feet in the corridor reached them. 'If that's you with the bloody trolley, Jenny, you're too late,' he barked without looking up.

There was a stony silence. Abby looked round—and found Sister glaring at them from the doorway. The room was a mess, with the bedding tossed on the floor and a chair overturned. The patient lay spreadeagled inelegantly on the carpet. And, worst of all, there was a gypsyish-looking man in jeans making a medical examination...

Two hours had passed. Two hours in which Abby and Sam had been herded from Sister Bradshaw's office to the Nursing Administrator's office and now to the most senior official of all, Mr Pringle, the Hospital Administrator. Mr Pringle's room was huge and deep-carpeted. He sat behind a massive chrome and glass desk, with an impressive array of telephones and a horribly modern painting on the wall behind him. Sister Bradshaw and the Nursing Administrator sat by the side of him. Abby and Sam stood in front of them. Abby couldn't help but stand to attention, the result of years of training, but Sam slouched with his hand in one pocket. When he had first explained his presence to Sister he had been bright and co-operative, but his mood had been deteriorating. As a

186

doctor he had to go along with the enquiry, but Abby could tell he hated being quizzed by bureaucrats.

'You do realise that you had no right whatsoever to even be in the hospital?' Mr Pringle asked. 'As for administering to one of our patients...' He tutted under his breath. Abby could feel Sam quiver with rage.

His voice, when he spoke, surprised her by its composure. 'If I hadn't been here you know as well as I do that Mr Drinkwater would probably have died. Perhaps as hospital administrators you would have preferred that, but as a doctor I know it's my duty to preserve life when I can.'

'To be frank, Dr Malone, that's quite beside the point.' Mr Pringle tried to smile at them but failed, managing only to show his teeth, as a dog does just before it bites. 'Mr Drinkwater was under the care of his specialist. He had arranged and paid a great deal of money to be seen by one of London's top consultants—and instead...'

'Instead he has to be resuscitated by *me*.' Sam gave a cynical laugh. 'Where is his specialist, by the way? Has he turned up yet?' Sister Bradshaw gave an embarrassed cough and shook her head discreetly in

Mr Pringle's direction. 'Do you think that when he does he'd prefer to find his patient alive, albeit because of me—or dead?'

'There's no point in pursuing this line of argument,' Sister butted in. 'Nurse Andrews, perhaps you would like to tell Mr Pringle why Dr Malone was in the hospital to begin with. He is a friend of yours, I take it?'

Abby glanced at Sam. His mouth moved almost imperceptibly, forming the word, 'No.'

'Yes, he is,' she said firmly. 'I knew that he was an experienced doctor, so when I found that Mr Drinkwater had arrested I had no hesitation in accepting his assistance—particularly,' she added, 'as there were no other senior staff and no equipment to hand. I have no doubt that he saved Mr Drinkwater's life.' Her pent-up head of steam ran out and she stood silently surveying her shoes.

'Your opinion was not solicited, Nurse,' Mr Pringle said sharply. 'The fact is that you are not permitted to receive personal visits while you are at work. Patients come to the Bentley to be certain that they will not be bothered or pestered in any way. We cannot have the staff rooms turned

188

into public meeting places.'

Watching the faces of the three senior members of staff, Sam gradually realised that they were in fact shaken by what had happened. They were being aggressive as a form of defence. They knew as well as he did that they could have had a disaster on their hands, but they would not admit it, because by doing that they would have undermined confidence in the hospital. This was stonewalling on a grand scale. The three officials put their heads together and talked quietly for a moment. Sam took the opportunity to reach out and pat Abby encouragingly on the shoulder.

'They're terrified in case word of this leaks out,' he muttered. 'Don't worry, everything's going to be fine.' Her eyes, so large and troubled, made him want to fold her in his arms and keep the world at bay. The fact that they should be taking this out on her, when she'd done all she possibly could to save the patient, made him even more mad than he'd felt on his own behalf.

'Nurse Andrews.' Mr Pringle turned back to them. 'You were aware, I'm sure, of the rules that pertain to receiving friends at the hospital, yet you seem to have done nothing to deter Dr Malone from staying. Since you have flouted that part of your contract, I'm afraid that we have no alternative but to dismiss you. You may leave this afternoon, and in lieu of notice of dismissal we will make you an allowance of one month's pay. As for you, Dr Malone, in view of the fact that Mr Drinkwater does seem to be making a satisfactory recovery, we won't take any action.'

Sam's eyes flashed. 'You won't? Well, I will! Nurse Andrews and I both belong to professional bodies who will take a very dim view of this afternoon's work. In fact the whole episode would make an interesting and thought-provoking feature for a newspaper...'

As one, Sister Bradshaw and the Administrators jumped to their feet. 'There's no need for that!' Mr Pringle cried. 'I think if you'll just take time to consider the situation, Dr Malone, you will realise that we have no other course.'

Sam swore. 'I can't understand why Abby wanted to work in a place like this to begin with—it stinks!' He shrugged. 'But then it's run as a business investment by business people like yourself, Mr Pringle, and you don't really give a damn about the patients so long as the money is rolling in, do you?'

Abby grabbed his arm, tried to calm him down. 'It's all right, it doesn't matter. I didn't want to go on working here anyway.' He shook her off.

'I demand acknowledgement from you that I saved one of your patients' lives—a written acknowledgement. And I also demand that you reinstate Nurse Andrews. If by chance she should not wish to continue working for you then I imagine that a significant amount of compensation would be appropriate.'

Mr Pringle and the Nursing Administrator eyed the pair in the middle of the room balefully but said nothing. They had obviously just recognised that they'd met their match. After a long pause, Mr Pringle nodded. 'All right, Dr Malone, we'll consider what you've said. We will, of course, be holding an internal inquiry into the matter. When that's been completed we will contact you. Meanwhile I hope that you'll observe a professional silence on the subject?'

'For a week,' Sam agreed. 'Then I'll start taking my own kind of action.'

'Don't be hasty,' Mr Pringle grimaced. 'I think until we've made our decision it would be better if Nurse Andrews were to take some leave.' He glanced dismissively in her direction. Abby nodded, shell-shocked by what had happened. Right now, she didn't ever want to have to come back to the Bentley again. There was a sour, nauseating taste in her mouth and her head was pounding. What would James say? Would she be able to get another job?

'I shall see you both before long.' Mr Pringle led them to the door. 'In the meantime, Dr Malone, you might like to reflect on the fact that the BMA doesn't recommend its members to interfere in situations outside their authority.'

Sam swore under his breath. Abby could feel him tensed up like a tiger at her side. She hoped he wouldn't make the situation worse by reacting foolishly. This was just the kind of thing he'd hate, of course, coming from the kind of unstructured organisation he was used to. How could he even begin to understand the way a modern hospital like the Bentley was run?

Back in the locker room he waited in silence as she emptied her things. She didn't want to return here, even if they offered her the job, so she might as well take everything with her now. In a strange way, one of her decisions had been taken for her.

'Are you furious with me?' Sam asked at last, helping her into her coat.

'No.' She smiled. 'Do you realise that if you hadn't come to see Jenny none of this would have happened?'

'Your patient would have died, but your job would have been secure.' He stared intently at her, the silver scar gleaming against the darkness of his skin. 'Is that what you would have preferred?'

'No, of course not.' She couldn't stop herself from reaching up and running her forefinger along the outline of his lips. 'What would I do without you, Sam?' And then, standing on tiptoe, she kissed him.

CHAPTER EIGHT

Sam stood still for a moment, then deliberately pulled back from her touch. 'I'm sorry,' Abby muttered, so quietly that he hardly heard it. She put her hands deep in the pockets of her coat and turned away, aware that she had broken some unwritten rule that he had established between them. What a pity it was that he hadn't told her about it. He had a way of making sure that whatever she did, resist him or run to him, she was always in the wrong.

'Shall we go and see James? We can tell him what's happened.' He walked beside her, keeping his distance, and his voice sounded gruff and strangled.

'You can go, but I'm not going to. Don't tell him about me being suspended, I don't want him worrying unnecessarily.' She stared at the daffodils that lined the sweeping path up to the clinic and hoped that the mistiness in front of her eyes would clear.

'It'll be a good thing if you *are* fired.'

Abby felt her self-pity turn to indignation. 'And why is that?' she asked. 'What's going to happen if James and I are *both* out of work?'

'I assure you that James's family won't let a Farris, or his girl-friend, starve. Anyway, you shouldn't have too much trouble getting back into Highstead,' said Sam, the soul of reasonableness. 'Be honest, Abby, and admit that this place—' he gestured back at the Bentley and seemed lost for words for a moment. 'It's not a hospital!' he exploded suddenly. 'It can't cope with anything more major than an ingrowing toenail. And it's a crying waste of talent that people like you and Jenny should be working there!'

Abby couldn't help laughing at his indignation. Despite the cool, sardonic front he liked to keep up, Sam was just as capable of going up in flames as anyone else. It made him human, when so much else about him made her doubt whether he had a heart. He wouldn't kiss her now because, with James dependent on her, she was a liability. What he wanted was a no-strings relationship, but with James in hospital and her future uncertain, she had more strings than a parachute. And right now she needed him more than she'd ever needed anyone before. Wasn't it just too cruel, too ironic, to be true?

'I suppose I could always come with you and Jen to Africa and do good deeds,' she suggested, shrugging. 'So the Bentley isn't too hot...so what, I'm a free woman now.'

'No, you're not.' Sam took her by the shoulders and almost shook her. How could he put her off once and for all? How could he persuade her that loving him wasn't a good idea? 'You're going to stay here, in Highstead, and look after James until he's better. You owe him that. For God's sake, Abby, don't start making things any more complicated than they are. I only wish I'd never met you!'

His last words ended on a cry of quiet anguish, and looking up at him, Abby saw him bury his face in his hands. He sighed into his palms and there was a deep, despairing sound. They walked on in silence, each deep in thought. They must have passed people; they must have crossed roads and climbed the hill—but Abby wasn't aware of it. All she knew was that she'd been rejected. Sam had wooed her in his own unique fashion, he'd won her heart, and now he'd rejected her before she'd had a chance to give it to him. In a quiet way she respected him for his strength in holding her away from him. With James in hospital and things backfiring all around, it would have been easy for them to get involved.

As they approached the block in which the flat was situated, she felt things begin to fall back into perspective. She still felt

196

dry-mouthed and unaccountably breathless when she looked at Sam, but she began to see that it was probably all for the best. 'You've got some important duty to perform, haven't you?' she asked as they entered the lobby and climbed the stairs to the flat. Abby hadn't really intended to come here, but James's place was more comforting than her own single room at the nurses' flat—and there were no curious occupants to demand explanations and go on and on about it.

'I'll have to be in central London by five.' Sam looked at his watch. 'There's time for a cup of tea before I have to go. We can at least steady our nerves.'

'Why, what are you going to do?' she asked, following him into the kitchen. He wore faded blue jeans, and his legs were long and straight and athletic-looking. Everything about him was lithe and spare; he was one of those men who looked perfectly at home with his body—not like James, who sometimes seemed surprised at the amount of space he took up.

'You don't want to know,' he grinned, filling the kettle. 'It's nothing spectacular or glamorous. In fact it's precisely the opposite.'

Abby prised open the lid of the biscuit tin. It was empty; Sam was obviously not bothering to keep house properly. 'You've got yourself a job cleaning the toilets on Charing Cross Station,' she guessed. 'Or you're a part-time bus conductor...'

'Wrong on both counts.' He opened a cupboard and threw her a packet of digestives. 'If you really want to know, you can come with me this evening. I'd be interested to find how you react.' He looked at her keenly, his head on one side. Now that they were back on a jokey footing it was easier to cope with what he felt when he looked at her. He wanted her so badly that it hurt. And the knowledge that he couldn't have her just compounded the pain. If he was wise he'd leave now, take himself away from temptation—but he was like a moth round a flame. Abby was tempted, and not just by the desire to be with him, though that was strong. If she stayed here at the flat she'd only brood about the afternoon's events. 'Okay,' she shrugged, 'I'm game.'

'Good. The first thing you have to do is change into your oldest jeans and a sweatshirt—or something you can wash easily.'

198

'It sounds as if it's something to do with decorating,' she guessed.

'Wrong again,' he laughed. 'You're not going to find out until you come along. I'll even buy you a drink afterwards. You might need one!'

But the idea of touching alcohol was, Abby thought a couple of hours later, quite out of the question. As she bent low over an ulcerated leg, trying to remove some of the dead tissue without hurting, the patient breathed whisky and meths fumes over her, making her feel sick to the bottom of her stomach. She cleaned up the area as best she could, squeezing into it some special gel that Sam had brought along with him. Then she dressed it as carefully as she could. In the surroundings of the night shelter, which had been recently opened for London's dossers and homeless, it was difficult to observe sterile procedures; in fact it was just a case of trying to be as clean and systematic as possible. 'There, keep that on for a week and it might help...' She couldn't help feeling dubious about whether her treatment would do much good, but at least while it was clean and covered the likelihood of infection was reduced. Quite whether the old bag lady understood what she'd said, she didn't know, but she smiled cheerfully at Abby as she collected her belongings and went off to find her bed for the night.

From the other side of the makeshift cubicles that had been rigged up behind the reception area she could hear Sam talking to another patient, a young man who was very depressed—almost suicidal, from the sound of it. Abby tried not to eavesdrop as she listened to her next patient's chest and his rasping cough, but she gathered that the man had come down from the north in search of a job, under the impression that jobs were much easier to find in London than in his own area. He'd had no luck, his money had run out, and now he was reduced to staying in places like this for the night. With no permanent address and no facilities for keeping himself neat and tidy, he felt sure that he'd never be able to find a job, and he didn't even have the money to go back home...

Abby tried to concentrate on measuring out the cough mixture for her own patient. There wasn't much she could do for him—a cough was the price you had to pay for sleeping out at night, and it wasn't helped by a diet of takeaways and handouts. The only way to really cure him was to put him somewhere warm and dry and feed him properly—and he would never stand for that as he told her himself. A knight of the road, that's what he was, he informed her. For more than twenty years he'd been travelling the country, going to the seaside and the countryside during the summer and coming back to town for the long cold winter. He was, in fact, a surprisingly amusing companion and kept her entertained while she gave him a vitamin shot. She felt her heart warming to him. It was easier to feel sympathy for someone like him than for the drug addicts and alcoholics who seemed to make up the majority of the shelter's clients.

Sam was asking his patient about the possibility of going home as she ushered her old chap out and called in the next. The man behind the curtain agreed that he had somewhere to go, but he had no money to get there.

'I don't know what I've done to my arm, dearie,' explained her next patient, holding it out for her to take a look at. 'I slipped over after Christmas when it was icy, down in that park place by the Embankment. It hurt a lot then, but it seemed to get better after a few weeks. The only problem is I can't move it.'

'I'm not surprised!' Abby exclaimed as she felt the wrist, running her fingers up the bone. 'You must have broken it when you fell. Wasn't it very painful?'

The man shrugged. He was a rough-looking piece of work, unshaven and none too clean, but his manner was pleasant. Again the tell-tale smell of booze, beer this time, hung about him. Maybe, with enough alcohol inside you, even a broken wrist was bearable.

'Did you go to hospital?' she asked.

'Did I hell!' he spluttered, suddenly indignant. '*I* know the kind of things they get up to in hospital! You wouldn't get me in one except in a wooden box...' He rattled on at length, with stories he'd heard about people being chopped up for spare-part surgery and terrible tales of what they could do to you.

'Are you okay in there?' Sam's amused voice floated through the thin curtain.

'I'm just hearing about what terrible places hospitals are,' Abby laughed. 'And after this afternoon I agree with every word of it!' She rotated the wrist again. Where the bones had knitted themselves together there was a large subcutaneous lump. The nerves and tendons would all be affected by it. 'If you've got a moment, would you come and have a look at this?'

The curtain was drawn aside and Sam stepped in and examined the arm too. 'You're lucky it healed as well as it did,' he told the patient. 'But if you want full use of it back you'll have to go into hospital.'

The man began spluttering again, but Sam stopped him with a sharp glance. 'I know you don't like the places, but it's either that or continue without the full use of your hand. It's that or nothing—we can't do anything for it here. Sorry, but that's the way it is.'

With a hurt look, as if they'd betrayed him by not being able to cure him then and there, the man gathered his bags and left.

Sam noticed the look of surprise on Abby's face and shrugged. 'There are some people who are happier *with* their problems than they would be without them. You've just got to accept that in this line of work. You can't force high technology and modern wizardry down people's throats.'

'All the same, it's rotten knowing that a few days in hospital and a couple of weeks in plaster would sort him out if only he'd got the guts to do it.'

'You're going to have to learn to stop making so many blanket judgements!' laughed Sam. 'That looks as if that's it for the night,' he decided, peering out to see if there was anyone else waiting for treatment. 'Was it too dreadful for you?'

Abby thought for a few minutes. The shock of actually walking into a place like this was enough on its own. Then discovering that Sam had established his own kind of clinic here and had been coming each evening for weeks was another blow. And discovering that he expected her just to muck in and treat patients herself had nearly left her speechless. But although it was smelly and not a bit like the Bentley, she'd enjoyed it. It was proper nursing; well, maybe it wasn't very sophisticated stuff, but it was good to actually get to work on someone's scalded arm or ulcerated leg, rather than just serving tea and bringing bedpans. 'No, it wasn't,' she said. She'd have liked to say more, but earlier this afternoon when she had expressed her true feelings he had rejected her. Now she'd have liked to tell him how much she admired what he'd done; how much she'd misjudged him in the first place. She would like to have told him that at last she'd really begun to understand his approach to medicine and people and life. Because here, among some of life's losers, she'd been able to appreciate why he'd been so short-tempered about James's lifestyle—the comfort and ease they took so much for granted. She'd resented his attitude at first, but the new-found knowledge that all the while he'd been coming here and, according to some of the other volunteers, helping out elsewhere too, blotted all the past out.

Embarrassed by her thoughts, she asked, 'What happened to your last chap? The one who was depressed?'

'He decided to go home.' Sam was packing things up, putting away the antibiotic cream and the cough mixture in the big bag he'd brought with him.

'I thought he didn't have the money,' she said thoughtlessly, handing him some unopened dressing packs. There was a long silence. Sam concentrated too hard on putting things away neatly. Abby nodded knowingly. 'You gave it to him, didn't you?'

'What if I did? It's nothing to do with

you.' His eyes were hard, but they softened when he saw that she wasn't about to tell him off. His mouth twisted in that roguish smile. 'It's the least I can do.'

He turned back to zip up the bag, and as he did so Abby reached over to put the last tube of eye cream into it. Their hands touched, and it was as if, in touching, some spark was lit. He fastened the bag slowly, without looking at her, then straightened up and reached for her suddenly, taking her in his arms and kissing her with such tender desire that Abby felt herself almost fainting in his embrace. She steadied herself against him, and for a moment he stopped kissing her. 'Sam, you're amazing,' she murmured. His lips touched her throat, moving up towards her ear. 'You're such a *good* man, despite all I've said about you.' She kissed him then, feeling the dark stubble of his cheek against her lips, tracing the silver line of the scar with her mouth. But suddenly she was aware that he had stilled, that he was pushing her away again.

'Abby, you've got to understand, there's nothing I'd like more...' He stepped back and ran his hand through his hair. A shadow had cast itself over his face; he had that troubled, tormented look she had come to fear. 'I can't do this. Not to James, or to you. A fine friend I'd be...'

'It's me who'll have to take the blame. It's my fault for—' she hesitated. 'It's my fault for falling in love with you, Sam. James can't blame you.'

He seemed to stare right through her for a while, then he roused himself and picked up the bag and his jacket and walked out. It was almost, Abby thought, as if he hadn't heard her. What had she said to make him behave like that? Distressed, she followed him out. Of course, he *had* heard her. Her words, her talk of loving him, had bitten deep. It was strange; although he'd been taking the responsibility for people's health, for their lives, for so long, he'd never before been faced with a situation where his own action would so profoundly affect the happiness of others. It was up to him, all up to him. He had the power to whisk Abby away from all this, to take her away from James if he wanted. He wanted her so badly he could almost bring himself to do it. Just now he'd been so tempted, so pleased with her... But there was one person in the world who needed her more than he did, and that was James. If James had been hale and hearty he would have had no compunction at all in stealing Abby from him. Now he was sick, vulnerable, and his needs had to come first, even if Abby didn't agree.

He chatted with the volunteers who manned the shelter each night, but his mind wasn't on what was being said. Dimly, out of one corner of his eye, he could see Abby waiting uncertainly for him, unsure of what to do. He couldn't be cruel to her and leave her to go home on her own just because her presence disturbed him so much. Neither of them could be blamed for the circumstances in which they found themselves, after all. If only they could talk! But talk was impossible. The more he found out about her, the longer he was with her, the more difficult it was to get her out of his head.

'Come on,' he said, crossing the shabby entrance area. 'You've had enough for one day. We'll go home now.' They waited for a bus in silence, like two strangers, and as they sat together on the journey back to Highstead, Abby was aware of the space that seemed to be yawning between them. 'I have to come back to the flat,' she remembered when the bus deposited them at the top of the hill. 'I left my handbag there and it's got my keys in it.' She didn't want him to think she was pressuring him, following him home when she had her own place to go to. He just grunted, and she felt embarrassment overwhelm her. She'd come out with it. She'd said it. She would leave James for him if he wanted her—and he'd just pulled away as if it meant nothing to him. It had been one hell of a day, she decided, as Sam put the key in the lock and opened the flat door. And it wasn't going to improve now.

From the living-room came the noise of the television. A familiar form was sprawled on the sofa. 'James!' Both Abby and Sam spoke at once, and stopped at once, leaving a questioning silence in the room. James sat up and grinned like a maniac at them, not seeming to notice the quick flush of guilt that passed over Abby's face, or Sam's fleeting frown.

'Where on earth have you two been?' the invalid demanded. 'I called you three times this afternoon and neither of you were in, so in the end I walked home.'

'They've discharged you?' Abby was aware that her tone wasn't quite as delighted as it should have been. After all, she was supposed to be the distressed fiancée; she should be thrilled, not disturbed, to find him here. 'Have they found out what's wrong?'

'That would be *too* much to ask,' he said, pulling a face. 'I've persuaded them to let me out temporarily, so that I can go along with the rugger team on their trip to Cardiff. I couldn't miss that.'

Sam walked over to the big armchair, gave James a matey pat on the back, and sat down. 'They're not going to allow you to play, surely?' he asked.

James was hardly listening. He was looking over the sofa to Abby. 'Aren't you going to come and give me a welcome home kiss, darling?' he asked. On shaky legs she walked over and bent to kiss him. He didn't seem to notice that she pulled back from him a split second sooner than she should have, nor that her smile wavered on her lips. He just held her hand, smoothed her hair, and patted the sofa, inviting her to come and sit beside him. Finally, when she was settled next to him and he'd placed his arm firmly around her shoulders, James turned his attention back to Sam's question. 'No, I can't play, but there doesn't seem any reason why I can't go and watch. I think they were all getting a bit fed up with me just lying there, and Barry Taylor who's been doing the tests is going on the trip, so I'll be well looked after.'

'And you'll have to go back to hospital as soon as you get back from Cardiff?' Abby asked quickly.

'You make it sound as if you want to get rid of me,' laughed James, and pecked her on the ear. Across the room Abby's eyes met Sam's. They glittered darkly, then he dropped his gaze to stare at the floor. She could feel her nerves bunching at James's touch—a touch she'd once welcomed so warmly—and hoped that *he* wouldn't be able to feel her flesh crawling. She angled herself so that she was facing him, looking into those open, honest eyes, the pale, slightly freckled face, the smile that told her he was so pleased to be back with her. But it didn't work. She remembered how she had gone home to her parents after her first term at nursing school and how, in just ten weeks, all her old school friends had become like strangers. In those ten weeks she had learned so much, changed so much, that she'd somehow left them behind. Or may be not left them behind; she'd gone off in a different direction. And she could feel the same thing with James now. He had been in hospital for two weeks, but in those weeks she had changed. She had decided to take a different path, a path he couldn't follow. Without the faintest trace of doubt, she knew that James was her past—her life with him was over. But how could she begin to tell him *that* when he sat holding her hand and beaming at her? When he seemed to rely on her more than ever?

'I'm going to make some coffee,' she said as brightly as she could. 'Sam and I have had one hell of a day at the Bentley. Sam'll tell you about it.'

'The Bentley? What's been going on?' James's attention was caught, diverted from her for a few moments, and Abby slipped away to compose herself in the kitchen. There was, of course, nothing she could do. She would have to muddle along for a while before she could tell James finally that it was over between them. And Sam had rejected her too. A pained chuckle of amusement escaped her at that thought. She was going to be left with nothing, she could see that. But anything would be better than *this,* she decided, going back into the living room with the coffee. If she had to keep this front up for long her heart would break.

'...so it looks as if Abby's going to be without a job,' Sam was saying as she carried the tray in.

'Good thing too,' she added. 'I hated it there.'

'No, you didn't! It was better than Highstead,' protested James.

'It was horrible—the patients were snobs and the place was run like some kind of supermarket,' she said flatly. 'And it certainly wasn't as efficient as Highstead—we saw that for ourselves this afternoon.' Her voice, she suddenly realised, was sharp and scathing. It sounded as if she was being rude.

'Abby's still a bit shocked by it all,' Sam interjected, trying to take some of the sting out of her words, but James was visibly surprised by them.

'If I'd known you felt that way I wouldn't have suggested that you work there,' he said with a frown. 'I always thought it had a very pleasant atmosphere.'

'That,' said Abby swiftly as she handed him his coffee, 'was because you were never there for more than an hour or two at a time. And they tend to treat doctors as if they were God's gift to the management...' She was aware of Sam's warning gaze upon her and stopped herself from saying any more. The sudden realisation of what she was doing came to her. She was trying to pick a fight with James. If she could be angry with him and he with her, she wouldn't have to feel so bad about the way she felt.

'Sorry. It really *was* a shock this afternoon. If Sam hadn't been there we would have lost a patient, and for no good reason.' James brushed her cheek forgivingly with his finger, then bent to pick up his mug. Abby watched how he used both hands to hold it. He'd never held it like that before. It must be a technique he'd learned in hospital for preventing any accidents. She felt a stab of pity, and glanced over at Sam, who was watching his old friend as if in a trance. His eyes were shadowed, inward-looking. She had no idea what he was thinking.

They sat in silence for a while. 'When is this Cardiff trip?' she asked at last.

'The day after tomorrow, for four days. We'll drive up on Thursday and come back on Sunday night. It'll make a change from lying in that hospital bed.' Abby smiled sympathetically. 'I'm sorry you can't come with us, darling,' James whispered, 'but on these rugger club outings it's all the boys together.'

Abby tried to look disappointed. 'Never mind, when you're better perhaps we can do something.' She hated herself for making those kind of false suggestions. If he had multiple sclerosis there might not be a time when he *was* better.

He reached out for a biscuit, took one and then, without warning, sent the plateful spinning to the floor. Sam moved swiftly to pick them up, but Abby saw James's face begin to crumple with frustration. The smile left his eyes and he buried his pale cheeks in his hands. 'Oh God!' It was such a quiet, despairing cry that she felt her heart stop for a moment. 'Abby, what are we going to do? What *are* we going to do?'

Sam stood up and silently left the room. There was a silence, then the distinct sound of the front door closing.

'James, I'm going to have to go.' Abby levered herself up from the sofa, casting off his arm, which had been draped round her shoulder, as she did so. James reluctantly looked up from the snooker match he'd been watching on television.

'Where are you going?' he asked, tugging her back down again.

'I told you!' she laughed. 'That just shows how much attention you've been paying me! Honestly, you come out of hospital and all you can do is watch TV...' She didn't mention that secretly she was glad he hadn't asked questions. The snooker match had been a godsend as far as she was concerned.

'I'm sorry, darling. It's the novelty of it. TV withdrawal symptoms are terrible. What with one set to a ward and lights out at ten-thiry there's hardly a chance to see anything decent.' Abby went out to the kitchen to collect her coat and bag and he followed her. 'Do you *have* to go?' He put his arms around her waist and squeezed her tight, but there was none of that old magic there; all she wanted to do was get away from him.

'Yes,' she lied.

'Why?' he looked at her mischievously. 'Anyone would think you were trying to avoid spending the night with me!'

'Don't be silly!' Her voice sounded shrill and guilty.

'I'm not being silly. Before I let you go you've got to give me one good reason why you have to go back to that horrible old nurses' flat,' he demanded, zooming in for a kiss. Abby ducked and he found himself kissing her eyebrow.

'My mother's going to phone me tonight,' she said lamely.

'But it's already gone ten-thirty!' he laughed.

Some quick thinking was required here, Abby knew. 'They're out in Australia again,' she lied. Her father's job in publishing often took him to the USA and Australia, and as her mother had family in Sydney she often accompanied him. It was a lie, maybe, but not a huge one. 'And Australian time is ten hours ahead of ours—that's why Mum will be phoning so late. She's calling to let me know when they'll be back.'

James sighed. 'I don't believe it! I get out of hospital, I look forward to nothing but being with you—and your mother comes between us!' He laughed. 'Give her my best wishes, won't you, and tell her what she's done. Maybe we could meet them from the airport when they get back?'

'They'll probably arrive when you're away in Cardiff,' Abby fibbed, picking up her coat and sliding her arms into it before he could stop her. 'Anyway, there's plenty of time tomorrow.'

James looked slightly crestfallen. 'Actually, I won't be around much tomorrow. There's a big conference on private medicine up in Birmingham. I'm going up there with Ian and a couple of the other people who do private work.' He frowned. 'Don't tell Sam, will you? He wouldn't approve. But it's useful to go to these things, get yourself known, meet people—that kind of thing.' There was an uncomfortable pause.

Abby knew what he was thinking. What was the use of making friends and meeting people if multiple sclerosis meant that you'd never again be able to operate on or treat someone? A great surge of sympathy and guilt swept over her and she turned back to him and gave him a hug. 'Whatever happens,' she heard herself assuring him, 'everything *will* be all right.'

'I know that.' He smiled, but she could see the fear still lurking in his eyes. Despite all his jokes and smiles, she knew he was frightened. 'And now,' he laughed, 'you'd better go, because if you stay here looking at me like that for much longer I'll have to lock you in the bedroom with me!'

Abby walked down the hallway to the front door. 'I'll see you some time in the next day or so, whatever happens,' she said as she let herself out. 'Maybe tomorrow evening.'

'I expect we'll be back very late,' was all James would say. Abby hated the way those words brought her relief. He was going to be away tomorrow, and off to Wales the following day. She was reprieved—for the time being, at least.

She was walking down the hill, deep in thought, when a dark figure approached her from the opposite direction. She looked up and found Sam staring at her in surprise. 'What are you doing here?' he asked.

'What's it got to do with you?' she responded sharply, annoyed by his accusing manner. 'Where did you slope off to, anyway?' She wanted to ask how he could have gone off and left her alone with James, but she didn't dare. There was something dangerous about him. He had that awkward glint in his eye that she knew of old.

He tilted his head to one side and grinned crookedly at her. 'I'd say you were feeling thoroughly guilty and angry with yourself. And it's not a very loyal thing to do, Abby, leaving your boy-friend all alone on his first night home from hospital.'

'You've been drinking!' She walked on down the pavement, hoping he wouldn't follow her, but he did.

'I've had a few drinks,' he agreed, matching her step for step. 'But that's only to drown my sorrows.'

'What have you got to be sorry about?' she asked sourly.

Sam was quiet. How could he tell her that he'd left her alone with James because he couldn't bear to see them together? Or that he had been drinking in the vain hope that he could wash away his feelings for her? He shook his head. 'You'd be surprised,' was all he said. 'Seriously, Abby, why aren't you staying with James?'

Abby felt bogged down in her deceit. She couldn't lie to Sam. Not only did he have an uncanny knack of knowing when she was holding something back from him,

220

but he'd also talked to her mother the other day when she'd rung James's flat, unaware that to all intents and purposes, Abby had moved out. In fact she'd have to admit her lie to Sam, so that if James said anything about Australia he wouldn't spill the beans. All in all, it was better to tell the truth—so she did. 'I didn't want to stay with him. You knew that, anyway. When he gets back from Cardiff I'm going to tell him...'

'Tell him what?' Sam whirled her round and fixed her with glaring eyes. 'You can't let him down, Abby, not because of me or anyone. I'll be gone soon, and things will be like they were before I arrived.'

'Oh no, they won't!' She pulled herself away, but he caught her coat sleeve and hung on to it. A passing man gave her a questioning look, as if he was wondering whether she needed assistance, so she smiled and allowed Sam to take her arm. The last thing they needed was a scene in the street. Instead of propelling her down the hill to the flat, he steered her down one of the roads that led to the Heath, that unspoiled area of grassland, with its ponds and coppices, that formed the heart of Highstead.

'I need to talk to you somewhere private, *now*,' he breathed in her ear, and though she knew it was madness to even listen to him, let alone go with him, she allowed him to take her on to the Heath. The moon was full and the grass was silvery, transformed in the moonlight. Here and there, in the distance, were figures, most of them in pairs or small groups, walking home or exercising the dog. There was no sound of traffic. Had it not been for the glow of lights that was central London, spread out before them, they could almost have been in the countryside.

They walked to a secluded bench and sat down, each silently absorbed in the scene and their own thoughts. It was Sam who spoke first. 'We're in one hell of a mess, you know.' He looked at her, then drew closer, so that she could feel his thigh against hers. 'You mustn't say anything that will upset James. Promise me that.'

'I can't.' Abby swallowed. 'This is fine coming from *you*, Sam! You were the first person to tell me I'd got it all wrong by agreeing to marry him. I don't love him, and that's all there is to it. He's going to have to find out sooner or later, and I'll try not to hurt him too much—but whatever you say, I'm not going to change my mind.'

His arm snaked around her shoulders and held her to him, his chin tucked into her shoulder from behind. She looked straight ahead, feeling his eyes sweeping her cheekbones, her nose in profile. She should shrug him away, she knew—but she couldn't. He was like fire in her blood; he just had to touch her and she was aflame. 'I'm sorry,' he murmured. 'It looks as if I'm going to cause you both a lot of pain. It would have been better if I'd never come.'

'That's not true.' Abby turned and found his lips only a few inches from her own. 'James has been so happy with you around.'

'And you?'

Abby studied his face. There were fine lines around his eyes, caused by laughter and squinting into the sun. She loved everything about him, from those lines to the scar that ran along his jaw. When it came to love, it wasn't the perfections that mattered—not the elegant nose, or the firm chin, or the strong, straight eyebrows. It was the imperfections that touched her the most deeply, the proofs of character and humour. A dozen men might share his profile, but only Sam had that tough, roguish but tender look. She buried her face against his leather jacket. 'You know I'm glad you came. You know exactly how I feel. I don't know why I do feel this way. You've been so nasty to me.'

He kissed her softly and whispered her name, entangling his hands in her hair and trying to make her look up at him, but she refused, almost frightened of what she'd see in his eyes. Rejection again? 'If you're willing, we could get ourselves into even more of a mess.'

'I think we've done pretty well so far, thank you,' she retorted.

'I'd like you to come away with me.' A sudden breeze caught the young leaves of the trees and whipped them into noisy rustling. 'Just for four days, while James is away. I want to be alone with you for a while.'

'Where would we go?' It would be wrong, she knew. It would mean betraying James completely—but she wasn't sure that she could say no.

'Anywhere—within reason. Do you have a passport?'

She raised her head and nodded.

'Well, come away with me, then. Just for a few days. That's all I ask.' He kissed her lightly on the forehead.

'We mustn't!' Her cry was lost on the wind.

'I'm not going to force you into anything, Abby. If you say no we'll forget the whole thing.' He kissed her again and smiled that earth-shattering smile. 'And maybe I should warn you that I *don't* intend it to be a platonic holiday!'

Abby felt herself melting into his arms. What on earth did she have to lose? Sam was all she wanted, and here he was offering her a chance to go away with him... So what was stopping her from responding? If only James wasn't ill. If only she could extricate herself from him without hurting him. But she couldn't live her life by if onlys. Somewhere along the line you had to decide what you wanted and defy the world to get it. If she didn't accept Sam's offer she knew she'd always regret it. She had to trust her own senses. 'Yes,' she said. 'Yes, I'll come.'

'Good.' Sam held her close. His pulse was racing. For a moment there he had thought she was going to refuse him. 'I'll make the arrangements.' They sat together on the Heath, safe in each other's arms, until the moon rose high and white overhead and the last light in Highstead had been extinguished.

CHAPTER NINE

'It's beautiful!' The water taxi scudded across the lagoon, sending up sprays of water that were refracted in the air like thousands of tiny rainbows. In the distance the towers of Venice became more and more clear, a shimmering mirage in the late afternoon sun. The rows of houses along the shore became more defined, some of them slightly dilapidated but all of them picturesque in the soft terracottas and greys characteristic of the city. Then the Grand Canal, with its palazzos and the red and white striped mooring poles of the gondolas. There weren't many of them to be seen, but then it wasn't the height of the tourist season. Standing next to Sam in the back of the boat, her hair tossed and tumbled by the wind, Abby looked up and found him smiling at her. Her heart rose to her throat—a heart full of a mixture of incompatible feelings. Love, guilt, uncertainty. He sensed her confusion and put an arm round her shoulders.

'Just enjoy it for what it is, Abby,' he said quietly. 'Forget James, forget Highstead. You're here with me.'

She could feel his thigh against hers as the motor-boat slowed down to go under one of the bridges and on, past the Ca'd'Oro, a beautiful lacework palace with wonderful arched windows. Then the Rialto came into view, the famous curve of the bridge with its double arcade of shops and faces peering down at them from the parapets. Abby could scarcely believe her eyes. It was so beautiful, the colours so soft and harmonious. Down every little canal that led off the main one she could see balconies and intriguing spots. And there was a kind of quiet about the place—no traffic except the waterbuses plying slowly up and down the canal, and their own taxi.

'That's the Accademia bridge.' Sam pointed it out as they approached. 'And here's our hotel.' The boatman pulled in at one of the mooring spots and put their luggage, Sam's old grey pack and Abby's small suitcase, on to the paving. Sam paid, exchanged a few words of thanks with him, then helped Abby step to safety. 'I didn't know you spoke Italian!' she said wonderingly as he picked up the bags and headed confidently off.

'I've got a smattering of half a dozen languages,' he said absentmindedly, looking about him. 'Including Swahili and Russian. This way.'

Their hotel was a small *pensione*, set off the narrow canal that ran beside it and protected by high walls surrounding a pretty marbled courtyard with a fountain and clematis already coming into bud. It was clean, light and simple—just like their room with its white marble bathroom and the ornate double bedstead against the plain whitewashed walls.

'Is it all right?' Sam glanced round. 'We can go somewhere else if you want something more splendid.'

'It's perfect.' Abby went to open the pine shutters that covered the window, filtering the light. There was a view of the Grand Canal looking south to another island with a massive church standing alone on it. 'It's just like *Brideshead Revisited*,' she murmured. Suddenly, alone with him, she felt nervous. He seemed so tall, so overpowering in this plain white room. He came to stand by the window and put his arms round her as if he knew what she was feeling.

'It's all right,' he said gently. 'Why don't we unpack, then we can see the paintings in the Accademia or go for a walk. If we go to St Mark's Square we can have a cup of tea while the orchestras play.'

'Have you been here before?' Abby leaned back into the firmness of his body. He held her still against him.

'Years ago, when I was a student. That's how I knew about this place.' They stood silently entwined, looking out at the view for what seemed like hours.

In the darkness a new sort of magic seemed to overtake the city. The elegant squares were bathed in the soft light of old street lamps which threw into relief the carvings and decoration of even the plainest houses. Brightly-lit windows cast pools of dappled shadow on to ancient cobblestoned streets and the ornate well heads that appeared every few hundred yards. It was tranquil, calm, quiet—just voices and the sound of children playing somewhere in the distance. Passing under one low archway they heard a man singing a Mozart aria. They stopped and paused just to listen for a few seconds, and in the gloom of the old arch Sam kissed her, so softly that she felt all her misgivings vanish. Whatever anybody else could say, this was right, she knew it with all her heart.

They had dinner at a restaurant near the Rialto, a long white room with walls crammed with paintings and elegant Italian couples dining, and then walked to St Mark's for coffee. The huge square with its grey and white marble slabs in their intricate patterns, the domes of St Mark's Basilica dominating one end, the soaring height of the Campanile and the Statue of Venice's famous winged lion stunned Abby into happy silence. It was too beautiful to be real; she felt as if she was living a dream. But it *wasn't* a dream. And she could make all her other dreams real, she knew, if she wanted. She just had to have the courage.

They walked back to the hotel in silence. Venice seemed to shut down early at night. By nine the restaurants were closing and people were heading for their homes. They walked slowly, hearing the soft sound of their own footsteps. Sam's arm around

Abby, her arm around his waist. The people who passed looked knowingly at them and smiled. The Italians, more than any other race in the world, know love when they see it.

All her fear of him had gone. She wanted nothing more than to prove to him that she loved him. 'Are you sure you want to go through with this?' he asked as they climbed the stairs to their room. 'It's not too late, Abby. I'm not going to force you to do anything you don't want to.' Sam wished he really felt that way. He wanted her so badly that he didn't know what he'd do if she told him she'd changed her mind. But she didn't. She kissed him boldly and ran her finger along the scar on his jaw.

He made love to her so slowly and tenderly that she couldn't prevent the tears of joy spilling on to her cheeks. His body, so lean and firm, was the source of almost unbearable delight. With him she felt alive as she had never done before; she felt a depth of passion that she had never experienced with James. Sam cradled her in his arms, caressed her, kissed away those tears, and she held him to her, marvelling at the smoothness of his skin, the muscular strength of his chest and arms. 'I love you,' she murmured as he kissed her, his mouth travelling down from her neck to her breasts and back again. Sam hesitated and held back his instinctive response, which was to tell her that he loved her too—that he had never known this feeling before. That at last he felt a wholeness that had been lacking for so long. But then James's plaintive cry echoed in his ears—'What are we going to do? What *are* we going to do?'—and he bit back the words. He could promise nothing. Smoothing her hair from her face, he kissed her again, and softly again, until she fell asleep in his arms.

The days that followed fell into a pattern, and Abby knew she had never been so happy before. They lay in late in the mornings, waking in each other's arms and making love until the noise of the impatient chambermaid outside the door roused them, reluctantly, to get up. The mornings were brilliant with pale spring sunshine, and the breeze which came in off the lagoon was so light that they could take a breakfast of brioches and coffee in one of the little cafés near the hotel. Then there was sightseeing to be done—the Doge's Palace and the mosaic splendour of St Mark's to begin with, followed by walks around the Custom House with its great golden statue and a ride on one of the waterbuses across the narrow strait to Palladio's church of San Giorgio Maggiore. They walked holding hands, with eyes more for each other than for the architectural marvels around them. Abby could scarcely bear to breathe or to talk, lest the spell was broken—because it seemed like a spell. It had to be some kind of magic, surely, that could leave her feeling like this. All she knew was that, now she had found it, she could never let it go. They stopped at Zattere for lunch, at a tiny restaurant set back from the promenade.

'Sam, I want to come with you when you go back to Africa.' Her words broke into the silence, the blissful separateness from the rest of the world, that had surrounded them all morning. 'I want to be with you.' She reached across the table and took his hand. He looked from her out to sea, where a schooner was making its way into the harbour.

He knew what he should say. He should explain to her that it was out of the question; that she couldn't just traipse after him to wherever he was posted. There was no time for holding hands in the kind of places he was used to working, no soft beds for making love. But he couldn't. 'We'll see,' he said quietly.

'I'm serious. I'll train for it. I don't care how long it takes.' Abby could sense that he didn't want to hear such things and wondered whether she'd gone too far. Last night she could have sworn he loved her. He'd been so tender, when he'd held her and whispered her name over and over again. He hadn't said it, but he'd shown it in every gesture. But now there was something troubled in his eyes and she noticed how his jaw was tensed. She was suddenly frightened. Perhaps she had trusted him too much. Perhaps he didn't want to be chased, particularly by a woman who had given herself to him so willingly.

Sam sighed and held the back of her hand to his forehead so that her fingertips tangled in his short hair. 'Let's not plan anything.' He leaned over and ran his thumb across her cheek, as if he was trying to memorise her face by touch. 'I'm not in a rational mood at the moment, Abby. I can't take any decisions—not when you're so near.' He smiled at her imploring look.

'We need time to think it all through carefully—and right now all I want to do is go back to the hotel and take you to bed.'

His touch seemed to ignite her like a match to a blue touchpaper. Whether she trusted him or not, she could not resist the sensual glitter in his eyes or the pressure of his thigh against hers under the table. All she wanted, whether he loved her or not, was to lie with him again, feeling the warmth of his body against hers. 'Come on, then,' she smiled. 'Let's go.'

It was Sunday morning and the bells of the city were calling all good Venetian citizens to Mass. A dozen sets of bells mingled, swelled, died and then rose in a clamour again, like music. 'We've got to get up,' sighed Sam. 'Come on, we've got a plane to catch.' But he hesitated, unwilling to climb from the warm bed which seemed to have been their home in the past few days. Abby groaned and rolled into the hollow he left, breathing in his scent on the pillow. If time could freeze now, her happiness would be complete.

Sam stopped and peered out of the cracks in the shutters. The weather was grey and misty, a total contrast to the crisp sunshine of yesterday. The buildings along the canal were shrouded in pale wreaths of vapour. Venice had changed overnight into yet another of its guises. Now it was mysterious, secret and melancholy. The sun picked out the beauty of its colours, the dancing water everywhere. The mist seemed to emphasise the shabby walls with their missing patches of stucco, the glory of the past, faded and sad. It was, he thought to himself, apt that they should be leaving on a day like this.

Abby watched him as he stood naked by the window, looking out at the world. He was more beautiful to her than any other man she had ever seen. And she knew him intimately. It almost hurt her to watch him like this, and she didn't know why. Something in her heart seemed to dread that she wouldn't see him again—but that was ridiculous, they were flying back to London after lunch, and there she would explain to James what had happened, ask him to forgive her. Then at last she and Sam could begin to start planning their life together.

She stretched languidly like a cat on the bed, and Sam turned and grinned his wonderful crooked grin. 'Don't do that,' he murmured. 'You'll tempt me to climb back in with you.'

Abby just smiled enticingly and stretched again, and with a groan he crossed the room to her and took her in his arms. How could he bear to do the thing he *must* do? He wanted to spend an hour telling her how much he loved her, making it clear to her why he was going to do what he had to. But it was better to be cruel. It was better that she should never know how he felt.

At last they managed to get up and shower together in the little marble bathroom. It didn't take long to pack. Abby hadn't brought much, and she took one look at the mist outside the window and reached for both her sweaters. There was just time for espresso coffee and pastries in the little café along the canal before they had to set out for the airport. This time they took the waterbus that set off from the quay near Harry's Bar, and they sat inside, protected from the wind and spray, watching Venice fade into grey behind. It was as if it had disappeared, vanished like a fairytale city swallowed into the white mist. It was, Abby thought, Sam's arm safely round her, a fitting kind of end to their weekend.

The mainland loomed up, ugly bridges and flat grey landscapes, industrial buildings and dual carriageways on which Fiats careered up and down. They'd come back to the real world all right. Who could possibly believe that out there, in the lagoon, there was a city that rose gracefully from the waves? A city of winged lions and gold-encrusted churches? Of delicate tracery, like lace—but carved from stone? Abby smiled and turned to Sam, but he was looking fixedly out of the window. There was something about him that worried her—the set of his jaw, she realised, and when he turned to her there was a hardness in his eye which she vividly recalled from that afternoon when he had first pushed his way into the flat and thrown up in the bathroom. The gentleness that it had taken her so long to discover in him had somehow gone again. She shuddered and leaned closer to him. He was an impossible man, and that was why she loved him. He had refused to discuss their future, or even give her an indication of what he had planned for them. 'In London,' was all he'd said when she raised questions, when she told him that whatever it took, she was going to make her life with him. 'We can talk about it later, but not here. It's just you and me here,' he'd whispered.

The boat moored near the airport, and the passengers piled out on to the quay and walked briskly to the terminal. It was a small, undistinguished building, more like a local airport than an international one, and it was packed, even though there were only two flights due to depart in the next hour, one to London, one to Paris. Sam held Abby back from the throng who were all trying to check their baggage in and led her to the small bar, where he brought them both a glass of wine. 'I'll be back in just a second,' he smiled, and darted off through the crowd. She could see him talking to someone, his dark head above the others around him. Then he disappeared. She sat alone, nursing her glass and keeping an eye on their luggage.

It was twenty minutes before he returned, and Abby had begun to worry. The two check-in desks for the London flight were quiet, and over the tannoy came a request for all passengers for their flight to proceed to the departure lounge. She looked round anxiously—and there he was, approaching, looking calm and inscrutable and unruffled. 'Sorry.' He raised his glass. 'I didn't mean to be so long.'

'I thought we were going to miss the flight!' she laughed. 'We *could*. We could stay here for ever, and no one would know where we'd gone.' She leaned over and kissed him on the cheek.

He looked at her so strangely, with such sadness, that he took her breath away. 'Come on.' She stood up quickly, not quite understanding her reactions. 'We've got to get the bags checked in.'

He placed a single ticket on the table, next to her passport. 'I'm not coming with you.' Uncomprehendingly she picked it up, looked at it. Her name was printed on it. She heard his words, but they didn't make sense. 'I'm not coming with you, Abby.' His hand was heavy on her shoulder and she turned, shaking her head, to him.

'I don't understand...' The words came from a long way off, as if someone else was speaking for her.

'I'm going to Paris. The headquarters of the relief operation is there and I'll find someone to stay with.' He tried not to look at her, not to respond to the pain that had shot across her face. 'It's for the best.'

'For the best? But we were going to sort things out with James, I was going to come with you on your posting... I was going to *be* with you...' People were watching them now, aware that something devastating was going on.

'It wouldn't work, don't you see, Abby? James *needs* you. In a couple of weeks' time I'll be posted to the middle of nowhere and you'll forget all about me.'

'Hasn't this weekend meant anything to you?' she asked quietly, and the tears had begun to course down her cheeks and she couldn't stop them.

'Of course it has.' He held her to him, trying to shelter her from the interested eyes all around them. The tannoy shrilled again, and this time it called their names in a tortuous Italian accent.

'Then why are you doing this to me? Please, Sam, come back with me. Don't go like this.' She looked up at him and saw the cold glint in his eye, that hard expression he had had when she'd first met him.

'No, I can't.' He silenced her protest. 'Nothing you can say will make me change my mind.'

241

'When am I going to see you again?' It was all too much to take in, like some terrible nightmare. Abby's thoughts flashed back to the way they had been this morning, the pleasure and joy that they had found in each other. Did it mean nothing to him? Could she love him so much and he feel nothing in return?

'I'll send you a postcard each Christmas, I promise.' He smiled and smoothed back her hair, and she saw the tenderness lurking, unguarded for a moment. 'And maybe in another seven years or so I'll come back and see you again.'

The tannoy barked its final request, and Abby noticed that Sam's name had been dropped. They had registered that he was no longer on the flight. It was just her they were waiting for now. He picked up her bag, walked over to the check-in and thrust it at the girl who was waiting there. She took Abby's ticket, ripped out the coupon and inserted a boarding pass. 'You must go straight through,' she instructed in heavily accented English, and Sam pushed Abby through the barrier.

'Go on, catch the flight. This is the only thing we can do,' he whispered hoarsely as she hesitated and turned back to him.

Abby held out her hands despairingly. 'You don't understand, Sam. I love you. You're all I want. Can't you hear me? I *love* you!'

The check-in girl was looking increasingly agitated. Sam dredged for something to say, something that would take her away from him. He couldn't lie; he *wouldn't* lie to her and say that he didn't love her, that was asking too much of him. 'Have I ever said I loved *you?*' he asked quietly.

Abby shook her head, dimly aware of the other girl taking her by the arm and trying to turn her in the direction of Passport Control.

'Well then,' Sam shrugged. 'Goodbye, Abby.'

They were kind to her on the plane, sitting her right at the front in a row on her own, so that people wouldn't pass her and stare as they walked to the back. Abby was dimly aware of a stewardess patiently doing up her seatbelt for her, and once the plane was airborne they brought her a miniature of Grappa and tried to persuade her to drink it. She didn't, though. The plane hovered over the airport, banking to find the correct course, and she stared down at the building below. Sam was

243

down there somewhere. Maybe he was already on board the other plane on the tarmac, destined for Paris. A spark of hope held out in her until they broke through the clouds. Perhaps he was only joking. Perhaps he was sitting somewhere at the back. But he wasn't. Below she could see the Alps, dark and rugged under their peaks of gleaming snow. She was flying back to London, to James. It was as if Sam had never existed.

CHAPTER TEN

How she got off the plane at Heathrow and back to her room in the nurses' flat behind the hospital, Abby didn't know. She could remember nothing of the airport formalities or the long journey on the underground back to Highstead. It all seemed to have happened automatically, without any effort. In fact it was a shock to find herself alone at last, without prying eyes watching her and whispered voices wondering if she was all right.

In a daze she unpacked and put her

244

overnight bag away without really thinking why she was doing it; and then she realised that she was still sticking to the subterfuge that she had been here, alone, all weekend. James mustn't find her with her bag still packed and its incriminating airport tags on it... The thought made her cry again, great tearing sobs that she couldn't control. What was she going to do? She felt helpless and lost, and she knew it was all her own fault. There was no room for self-pity. She had knowingly fallen in love with Sam; she had knowingly rejected James for him. And she had known all along that Sam wasn't the marrying kind, not the type to settle down. James had warned her about that even before she'd met him, and still she hadn't listened. She had fooled herself into believing that he loved her as much as she'd loved him. *Have I ever said I loved you?* His words haunted her. No, he'd never said that. James was the one who constantly declared his love, not Sam.

Abby drew the curtains, though it was only late afternoon, changed into James's old tee-shirt and climbed into bed. She was tired; she hadn't had much sleep the past few nights. The thought made her cry again, and eventually she dozed off.

It was around eight-thirty when she was woken by the presence of someone else in the room. She turned over and switched on the bedside lamp, disorientated for a few moments, not sure if the past few days had been a dream. For one incredible moment as she looked up at the figure standing by her bed, she thought it was Sam; she *believed* for a split second that it was him. But it wasn't. It was James, and he saw how her face fell, how her look of joy turned to one of disappointment as she registered him.

'One of your flatmates let me in,' he explained, suddenly embarrassed. Something had changed between them, he knew. Abby wasn't the same as she had been before Sam arrived. A feeling of uncertainty overtook him. 'You weren't at home and Sam's not around. I just wondered if everything was all right.' He sat down gingerly on the edge of the bed. 'You don't look very well,' he added. In fact she looked awful. Her eyes were red and strained and her cheeks were blotchy. A few weeks ago he would have just taken her in his arms and given her a cuddle, but now he felt a gap yawning between them, and he didn't know how to bridge it.

'I'm *not* very well.' Abby tried to brush the hair from her eyes, but strands of it were stuck to her cheeks where she'd been crying. 'Sam's left, James. He's in Paris by now.' She sniffed.

James's mouth fell open; much as she despised clichés, Abby thought that he really did look like a goldfish. 'He didn't tell me he was going!'

'He didn't tell me, either. Not until the last minute.' She tried to laugh—after all, it was painfully true—but found herself choking on a sob.

'You didn't have a row, did you?' James looked at her curiously. 'Is that why you're so upset? I thought you'd be pleased to see him go. Only a few weeks back you were trying to get rid of him.'

She shrugged as nonchalantly as she could. It was difficult when that numb black hole of despair was eating away at her insides. 'We didn't have a row exactly. I suppose it was a difference of opinion—yes, you could call it that. He'd been called back to Paris for news of his next assignment, so he decided to go sooner rather than later. I know he was sorry not to be able to say goodbye to you properly,' she invented. 'He sends his love and said he wanted to hear how you were doing.'

James looked bright again. 'Actually, one of the reasons I came round was to tell you that we may have got a lead on my problem. We met this guy who's being doing some research on implants...' He proceeded to explain, but after a minute or two it became obvious that her thoughts were elsewhere. Somehow, although she was looking at him and seemed to be hearing, he knew that she wasn't taking in what he was saying. There was a glassy brightness to her eyes that frightened him. He didn't seem to be able to communicate with her any more.

'You're not listening, are you?' he said, trying to make it sound like a joke.

Abby shook her head. 'I'm sorry, I don't know what's wrong. I think I'm going down with the 'flu or something. What were you saying?' She smiled too sweetly at him.

'Doesn't matter—it can wait a while. It may be just another wild goose chase.' He looked at her curiously. 'Would I be right in guessing that you got quite fond of Sam? You seem very upset about him going away.'

Abby swallowed. How could she begin to tell him how fond she'd become of Sam? And now wasn't the time to break the news. Maybe, now he was gone, it would be better if James *never* knew what had happened between them. 'He grows on you,' she admitted grudgingly, trying to behave in the way that she thought James would expect her to. 'I didn't like him at all at first—he was so pushy. But he does have a certain charm. I'd got used to having him around, I suppose.'

James watched her eyes filling with tears and passed her the box of tissues on the bedside cabinet. 'You've had a tough time recently,' he comforted. 'First Sam, then me going into hospital, then losing your job and Sam just walking out. I'll make it up to you soon, I promise.' He put his arm round her, but she just cried all the more. James was baffled. He seemed to be able to do nothing right these days. At one time he'd thought he understood her; he'd felt so close to her that he'd really believed he could read her mind. But now... 'Do you remember that night I came back from rugger and we looked Sam up in the photo album and I told you all about him? I told you he was a good guy, didn't I? But you didn't believe me when you met him.' He smiled. 'You even insisted on moving back here because you wouldn't share the flat with him—and now just look at you, Abby! I told you he could talk the birds down from the trees, but you wouldn't believe me...'

He laughed softly to himself, amused that she, like so many others, had been deceived by Sam's appearance and manner. Good old Sam. The nurses who had complained about him while he was their patient now sang his praises; he'd become a kind of myth at the hospital. Awkward, obstinate, difficult but with a quality that overcame all that. James wished that, whatever it was, he could have it too, but he'd recognised years ago, when they were students together, that there was something special about Sam Malone. Perhaps it was charisma; he seemed to win people, all kinds of people, over. And despite her initial fight, he'd obviously won Abby over too.

'Come on,' he hugged her. 'He'll be back one day. And meanwhile you've got me.' It was a joke, but it seemed to make her cry all the more. 'Abby! Please, tell me what I can do to make you feel better,' he pleaded.

'Nothing.' She patted him reassuringly on the knee and tried to hold back a sob that insisted on rising in her throat. 'Honestly, I don't know what's wrong with me, James. I'm sorry. I think maybe I just need a couple of aspirin and a good night's sleep.'

He kissed her gently on the cheek and got up. 'All right, I'll take the hint. Can I make you something to eat before I go?' She shook her head. 'Okay. I'm going back into hospital for tests tomorrow morning. They may let me out or they may want to keep me in for a couple of days. Will you keep in touch and come to visit me?'

'Of course I will,' she sniffed, meaning every word of it. He was so sweet, so kind—and so lacking in suspicion. His generosity made her feel all the more guilty. He blew her another kiss and closed the bedroom door.

'Well?' Jenny looked up expectantly as Abby slid into a seat at the table. 'Who did you see?'

'Mr Pringle and Sister Bradshaw.' Abby ordered a cappucino from the waitress. 'They offered me my job back. It seems that once they got over the initial shock they changed their minds about firing me. They were even prepared to thank Sam personally. I had to tell them that he'd gone and couldn't be contacted.'

'And will you go back to work there?' asked Jenny, stirring her own coffee.

'I don't want to, but a girl's got to live... How about you, anyway? I haven't seen you for ages.' Abby didn't want to talk about herself. Jenny knew her too well to be fooled by false smiles.

'I've got my place on the course. Look!' From her bag Jenny pulled a file of papers and prospectuses. 'Here we are.' She took a letter of acceptance out of its envelope. 'I begin at the end of May for three months. It's not exhaustive, but it gives you the basics of tropical and emergency medicine and it's aimed at preparing you for the kinds of conditions encountered in the Third World. I'll have to brush up my midwifery, too, by the looks of things. If I pass the course I could be sent off in August—it's exciting, isn't it? And just think, I might bump into Sam! Abby, are you all right?' She peered curiously over the rim of her cup. 'You've just gone the colour of a Bentley sheet—so white you're almost blue. Are you feeling okay?'

'Yes, just a goose walking over my grave.' Abby tried to distract her. 'Do you get paid while you're on these training courses?'

'Yup, same rate as we'd be on if we were at Highstead Hospital, plus travel allowances—there's quite a lot of trips and possibly a couple of weeks to be spent working away from home.' Jenny grinned. 'I'm so pleased I made my mind up, otherwise I could have gone on mouldering here for years.' She shoved the papers in Abby's direction. 'Why don't you have a look through them too? I know you hate the Bentley, and I can't believe that you really want to go back to Highstead. And I know Sam thought you were the right kind of person to go and work abroad.'

'Did he tell you that?' Abby raised a cynical eyebrow. 'I volunteered to once, and he as good as turned me down. As far as he's concerned, my place is right here, propping up James and the private health system.'

'That's not what he really thinks— *thought*. You two always seemed to be at loggerheads, though, didn't you? If he'd told you what he really thought of you you probably wouldn't have believed it.'

Abby pulled a face. If only Jenny knew quite how much Sam had kept from her—like the fact that he didn't love her, no matter how much he'd seemed to. In the three days since she'd got back from Venice she'd been through a lot. First of all that sharp pain of betrayal, then the dull, empty feeling of despair—and now just that quiet ache as her heart began the healing process of forgetting him. Not that she could ever forget him; she couldn't even begin to try. But maybe one day she'd be able to think of him without pain.

'You know, it wouldn't take much to persuade me that you'd fallen in love with him.' Jenny fixed her with a piercing mock-Svengali-like gaze. 'Oh, my God! Abby...you poor thing. And what about James?'

Abby held her hands to her face and peered into the frothy cream on top of her coffee. It was no good trying to lie to Jenny, she'd always known what was going on.

'James doesn't know, and I don't want him to. *Please*, Jenny, not a word. I've been offhand enough recently to him, and he's always been so nice...'

'That's half the problem with James,'

Jenny sighed knowingly. 'He's too nice for his own good. So what are you going to do? Stick with him? You know what I feel—I thought you should have refused even to get engaged to him in the first place. He'll make someone a marvellous husband, but not you.'

'I don't have much alternative. You know, I haven't told a soul about this, and I feel so much better just having admitted to you what's been going on.' It was true. The relief of being able to share the problem was immediate. Abby could feel some of the tension beginning to seep from her. 'To be honest, Jenny, I thought you'd fallen for Sam, too.'

Her friend blushed, then said, embarrassed, 'Of course I did, just like every other female who clapped eyes on him. He knew what was going on, of course, and made it perfectly plain that he wasn't interested. I didn't like it very much, but at least he was honest, and at least he took a friendly interest in me, and he didn't have to do either.'

They sat silently for a few moments, Abby studying the traffic that passed outside the window. The café they were sitting in was only a short walk from the

Bentley. They'd arranged to meet here when Abby had received her summons back to the hospital.

At last Jenny spoke. 'So we've both been disappointed by the great Dr Malone—you more than me, perhaps. Now we've got to pick ourselves up, recognise him as the rolling stone he is, and go on with our lives. And you still haven't told me what you're going to do about James.'

Abby smiled, the first spontaneous smile she'd managed for days. 'I'm not going to marry him, that much I do know—though how I'm going to get out of it I'm not sure. And I can't go calling it all off while he's in a hospital bed. So for a while I'm just going to have to wait and see. I'm going to have to go soon, too. Visiting time is almost up.' She checked her watch.

'What about the Bentley?'

'I don't think I could bear to go back. There are other nurses who do better in places like that than me. When are you leaving, anyway?'

Jenny threw her hands in the air in joy. 'The end of the month, and I'm having a party to celebrate. I thought I'd have some holiday and maybe go and stay with my family for a while before I start the training course. After all, if I get posted abroad immediately it may be some time until I see them again.'

Abby shook her head wonderingly. 'You've got everything so beautifully worked out. I envy you, I really do.'

'In that case, take these with you.' Jenny piled the papers and folders together and pressed them into Abby's hand. 'Go on, reading them won't do any harm.'

Abby was still holding them when she arrived on Men's Medical to see James. He was perched on the side of his bed, fully dressed, and as she approached he beamed at her and walked to greet her. He was so excited that the whole ward must have heard his announcement. 'They've done it, Abby! They've cracked it! You won't believe it!'

'Done what?' His pleasure was infectious. For a moment she forgot Sam. 'James, calm down a second! What's happened?'

'I'm better—or I will be in a week or two. It's all so obvious—that's why everyone overlooked it.' He grabbed her by the hand and made her sit on the bed as he gathered his things. 'I'm coming home with you now, and with a bit of luck I'll never have to come back—as a patient, that is.'

'Stop it for a minute and tell me what they've done! You're talking strangely... What's wrong with your mouth?' she asked suspiciously. Surely the muscular control of his jaw wasn't beginning to go? She realised with a jolt that despite it all she *did* care deeply about him. She didn't want to see him suffer. She felt for him as she might a brother; concern, care, but nothing more. It was strange how quickly strong feelings could vanish. Just a month ago she would have sworn that she loved him. Her heart gave a warning contraction. No, maybe at that time she hadn't known what love was. She'd mistaken James's wonderful boyish care for her for love. But it could hardly compare with what she felt for Sam even now. If James had walked out on her she would never in a million years have felt the yearning desire for him that she did for Sam.

'It's my teeth—it's been my teeth all along. Do you remember that after Christmas I had quite a few of them filled?' James looked at her expectantly, and Abby nodded. She couldn't have sworn *when* he'd had them done but certainly not long ago. 'Well, they've been the cause of the problem. The amalgam they use to fill teeth contains quite a lot of mercury. If you're sensitive to it and you have lots of teeth filled with it you can be poisoned, and mercury poisoning has all the symptoms...'

'Of multiple sclerosis!' Abby sat back on the bed, gasping and almost overcome with relief. 'Oh, James! And we never even thought about it! And all this time they've been poking and prodding you and taking your blood—and it was your *fillings...*'

'It's good news, isn't it?' He gave a wry smile. 'I'm glad you're pleased.' Abby was aware that his mood had changed. He was quiet, and he was looking at her pensively. She suddenly realised that they were sitting at opposite ends of the bed, with three feet of clear space between them. And they hadn't kissed or even so much as touched. James looked uncomfortably at the pale green bedspread. 'You see, I'd begun to wonder if you'd rather I spent the rest of my days in hospital.'

The man in the next bed, who had been watching with a big smile on his face, seemed to sense that he wasn't wanted and rolled over, turning his back to them.

'How can you say that? Of course I wanted you to get better!' Abby was stunned, and her amazement showed.

'I'm sorry, I didn't mean to put it quite as brutally as that,' James faltered. He gazed at her and she could see the confusion in his eyes. 'What I meant to say was that something doesn't seem to be right between us. Something's changed, hasn't it?' He sighed heavily. 'A few months ago we'd have been doing a jig around the ward to celebrate, and now you're sitting on the end of my bed, like someone I don't know very well...'

Abby slid along the bedcover so that she was closer to him, but he put out his hands to stop her. 'No, honestly, Abby, you don't have to pretend. What's happened? Was it Sam? When I got home after seeing you in the flat the other night I was so surprised by it all—him going, you being so upset—that I didn't really think. But I've had plenty of time in the last few days to put two and two together.'

She nodded before he could go on and spell out what it was her job to say. 'I'm sorry. You don't know how sorry I am. But you're right, it *was* Sam. I fell in love with him, just like all the other women who met him. And if it's any consolation,' she added, watching his face, so open, so honest, fall like a stone, 'he just walked away from me like he did from everyone else.'

It was her turn to stare miserably at the bedspread now. 'I see.' James bit his lip. He'd tried to convince himself that it couldn't be true, but there was nothing like bedrest and occasional trips to X-Ray and the labs to allow the mind to wander and work out things it might not normally probe. 'I suppose what I really need to know is whether there's a chance that we could—' He stopped and looked at her questioningly.

'I don't think there is. James, it's my fault. I know you won't find it easy to believe it, but it happened without any encouragement on my part. I didn't like him, you knew that. And then somehow, for some reason...'

'It's all right. Well, it's *not* all right,' he contradicted himself, 'but I think I do understand. That's not to say that I don't love you, Abby. I do; I'd marry you tomorrow if you'd let me.' He thought for a moment. 'There's something you should know, I suppose. All this has happened before. Do you remember when I first told you about Sam and you wanted to know why we'd gone our separate ways—why we'd been friends and then suddenly he'd gone off and I didn't go with him?'

She nodded. 'Yes.'

'It was because he stole my girl-friend.' James gave a rueful laugh. 'It's true. I was going out with a girl—I don't even remember her name now—and Sam came along and bang! I don't think he even had to try much; she just took one look at him and waved me goodbye...'

Abby felt the emptiness inside her growing, a gnawing despair that she couldn't prevent. 'And now I've gone and done it too!'

He reached out and touched her wrist comfortingly. 'At least you're still here. I don't know what I'd have done in the past weeks without you. But let me finish that story about Sam. I think he got tired of her after a while and he wanted to make it up with me and be friends again. I wouldn't speak to him—when you're twenty you think you'll never get over something like that. It was the old story of best friends betraying each other and turning into arch-enemies as far as I was concerned.'

'And that's why you gave up your idea of doing the kind of work he does,' said Abby, almost to herself.

'That's right. By the time my pride had recovered he'd taken off and I didn't even know where he'd gone. So I started my career in this direction.'

'And those postcards?'

'A typically Sam reminder that he was still alive—and maybe sorry for what he'd done. Over the years of course I forgave him and wished like hell I'd never been so furious with him in the first place, but by then it was too late. And then I came home that night and there he was, in bed—'

'And I disliked him so much that I'd cheerfully have kicked him out in the snow. Oh, James, we're crazy!'

'No, we're not crazy. It's just the effect he has on people. I told you from the very beginning that there was something special about him.' James shook his head. 'If I'd thought he'd do it again I'd never have left you two in a room together. As it was, you seemed to hate him and he didn't seem so keen on you. And I thought that after what had happened last time he'd have the intelligence not to let it happen again.'

'I don't think he wanted it,' Abby

confessed, remembering the times he'd rejected her advances, his words about not coming between them. 'He felt bad about it—and I pushed him.' She took James's hand and grasped it hard. 'I'd do anything to go back to the way we were before he arrived, but it's too late. And it's my fault. If only I'd known what you just told me I'd have understood what was happening. As it was, I wouldn't take no for an answer.'

James looked down the ward, and his eyes seemed to have a glazed sparkle about them. 'Perhaps we've both grown up a bit in the last few weeks,' he said at last. 'Certainly I've had time to think about what I want to do with my life. For a while I thought I wasn't going to have much option. I was beginning to believe what everyone else thought—that it wouldn't be long until my life was seriously affected by MS. Now I've got a reprieve I still think I'll go through with my decisions.'

'What were they?' asked Abby.

'I'm not terribly happy living in London, so I thought I'd go somewhere in the country. Not lambs in the fields, perhaps, but somewhere less smothered in carbon monoxide fumes. Somewhere you can bring up children.' He coughed. 'Forget that last bit. Am I going to see you around, Abby?'

'Yes—if you want to, that is. Honestly, James, you still mean a lot to me. Perhaps, one day, we can get back to the way things used to be. But meanwhile, we can be friends, can't we? It would be a way of proving to Sam that he can't ruin everything.'

'That's good.' James extricated his hand and stood up to collect his overnight bag. 'I'm going back to the flat now, and then I'll have a few days with my parents. Maybe when I get back to town we can have a drink together?'

'I'd like that,' Abby smiled. Why she couldn't love him as she did Sam Malone she didn't know. He must surely be the kindest, most gentle man on earth. Perhaps she didn't deserve him; yes, that had to be true, she told herself as she watched James walk down the ward and into Sister's office. Picking up her handbag and papers, she followed him out. But instead of walking the short distance back to her own flat, she turned up the road and headed on to the Heath. She didn't know where she was going and she didn't really care. Over on the top of one of the hills a man and his son were flying a kite, which bobbed around in the spring breeze. A labrador chased a ball across her path and came up, tail wagging, to be stroked. She fondled his ears absentmindedly until his owner called him away. Then she realised where she was. Behind a small covert of trees there was a bench, fortuitously empty. The bench she and Sam had sat on that night they'd got back to find James waiting for them. The night that Sam had suggested the trip to Venice.

In the daylight the worn wood with its covering of carved graffiti looked less romantic than it had by the light of the moon and stars, but she sat down nevertheless, and cast her mind back. It was painful, and she began to realise just how much of it she had blocked out. She had tried not to think of their nights together, of him in her arms, the passion of their love. It was like a dream, but as well as hurting, it also gave her back that sense of joy she'd experienced with him. James's story about how this had all happened before ran through her mind, and so did one comforting thought. Maybe

Sam really cared for her, and for James. Maybe that was why he'd refused to let her go with him, because he knew it would be best—and not for his own selfish reasons. Perhaps, somewhere in Paris, he was sitting feeling the same kind of emptiness and wanting that she was experiencing. It was a stupid idea, she knew that really, but it made her feel better. And now she had to make up her own mind what she was going to do. The world was her oyster, for a while at least. If she didn't accept her job offer at the Bentley she could look forward to a decent lump sum from them in lieu of notice and in order to keep her quiet. There was no need to rush into anything. She turned over Jenny's folder of papers in her hand and started reading.

CHAPTER ELEVEN

Highstead Hill was pulsating in the summer heat as Abby and Jenny jumped off their bus. The plane trees were beginning to wilt and the tarmac of the road was sticky. Jenny pushed back her hair from her perspiring brow and laughed. 'They said nothing about acclimatising us on this course, but we seem to be getting it thrown in for free! It must be in the nineties! Can I come back and have a drink at your place before I toil home?'

'Of course you can.' Abby suddenly remembered. 'You can't stay too long, though. I'm off to town this evening.'

'James?' asked Jenny.

'No, not James. I only see James once a week at the most. I don't want to encourage him.' They walked slowly down the roads that led behind the hospital to Abby's flat. The streets were deserted. For nearly a fortnight now it had been like this—almost too hot to move. Sensible people had taken their summer holiday while they had the chance. London was full of bewildered tourists who had come clutching pacamacs and umbrellas, but not many natives.

'Have you done your homework for tomorrow?' Abby asked as she let them into the flat. Someone had left the curtains drawn, so although the place was stifling it was at least dim, a pleasant change from the glare.

'Of course!' Jenny made her way to

the kitchen and began running the tap. 'If you want to cheat and borrow my answers you can. I can't remember what the calculations came to, but I've got them written down somewhere in my notebook.'

'I've no intention of cheating—I just wanted to see if they tallied with mine, that's all.' Abby opened the fridge. 'You can drink lukewarm tapwater if you want, Jen, but I'm having iced water from the fridge.'

Jenny grabbed the bottle and held the freezing glass to her arms. 'That's wonderful!'

'You're supposed to drink it,' Abby commented dryly, taking it back and fetching glasses. 'We can sit in the garden if you want to improve your tan.'

There were two tatty deckchairs already out, and a couple of dozing nurses stretched out on towels in the parched grass. Officially it was the domain of the ground floor tenants, but no one seemed to mind who used it. They hitched up their skirts and exposed their bare legs to the sun.

'Do you think you're going to be able to cope?' Jenny asked casually, closing her eyes. 'I sometimes wake up screaming in the night, thinking of malaria and green monkey fever and bilharzia. Perhaps we're both nuts, volunteering for this kind of thing.'

'I feel the other way,' Abby murmured sleepily. She went to push back her hair from her shoulders and suddenly remembered that it was no longer there. She'd had it all chopped off. Everyone had told her she was stupid to do so, but she'd wanted some kind of outward sign that she'd decided to change her life. James had told her that losing her hair was a penance. Jenny had told her that it was a sign of grief. Well, she'd had something to grieve for, and to feel guilty about. And short hair was certainly an advantage in this weather. 'The more I begin to understand, and the more I realise I can do, the fewer doubts I have about it all. I used to wonder what one nurse could do among all that poverty and disease. In fact I used to wonder whether people who volunteered to go out to the Third World weren't just doing it to salve their consciences and make themselves feel saintly. Now I'm beginning to see just how much a single person *can* help.'

Jenny muttered something, but she was

already half asleep. Abby lay there for half an hour with her, before getting up and going in. Jenny was already tanned; there was no danger of her getting burned now that the sun was beginning to sink. In the flat she showered and changed into one of her old cotton skirts and a tee-shirt. Then she ran her fingers through her hair, which was already dry, and set off again for the bus stop. The traffic was slow and tempers were fraying. Down the Euston Road a car had collided with a taxi and the two drivers were having a fight in the middle of the street. Abby got off and walked.

It was odd how many changes you could undergo in such a short time, she thought. Three months ago and it had seemed that her world had come to an end. Now here she was doing things that she'd never have dreamed she could cope with.

She turned off Tottenham Court Road and threaded her way through a maze of streets before arriving at the open doors of a large converted warehouse. Some of her regular customers were already seated on the pavement in the heat; bag ladies and men, young homeless people who'd come to London looking for jobs and found nothing, and people who could not, or would not, fit in with society's way of doing things. One or two of them greeted her as she walked in.

'Hello, Abby!' a voice hailed her from the gloomy coolness of the warehouse. She waved back at Steve, the young man who ran this place. He'd been friendly with Sam at the old night shelter, and when he'd tried to contact him to ask if he'd help out here she'd explained why he wasn't available and nervously asked if she could help instead. Of course, she was no match for an experienced doctor, but most of the people who came here didn't really need a doctor. Before she had started her training course with Jenny she'd helped out here during the day. Now she just came three times a week, in the evenings, giving what advice she could.

Steve was tall and bearded and handsome. Abby liked the way he dealt with people and his ability to care for even the most difficult of those who stayed. He walked across the reception area to her now. 'Not many tonight. I doubt if you'll have anything to do at all—except the odd case of sunburn, maybe!' He laughed. 'Anyone with sense will be sleeping out by the river or in the parks—that's if they haven't already left town.'

'I've brought the calamine lotion just in case,' Abby smiled, patting the small backpack she carried with her. It contained the things she needed, including her own stethoscope.

'I'm free this evening. Will you come for a drink when you've finished?' he asked. There was an edge of shyness in his voice that amused her. He could deal with belligerent drunks and turn out people he suspected of being on drugs, but when it came to asking her for a drink he was suddenly reticent.

'That'll be lovely,' she said. 'I'll give it until nine, shall I?'

He wrinkled his nose and pointed in the direction of the people sitting on the front wall. 'I shouldn't even hang around that long if I were you. If no one comes in for an hour I think you might as well call it a day.' At that moment two more people arrived and he went off to book them in. In April, when she'd first started coming, the place had been packed out every night and they'd had to turn people away. Now that the weather had improved and many of them were on the road again, they had scarcely half the sixty beds filled.

Abby went to her cubbyhole, which really was a converted cupboard, and laid out her bits and pieces. She bought her own bottle of sterile water and dressings. The charity which ran the shelter made a contribution to her expenses, but she didn't charge them for everything. Despite Steve's prediction, she had two patients. The first, she diagnosed, had sunstroke. He was feverish and sick and when questioned admitted that he'd been sitting in the sun in Covent Garden all afternoon, drinking. Abby sent him off with another volunteer to have a cool bath and something non-alcoholic to drink. He wasn't very badly affected; she'd see how he was in an hour or two's time. The second patient hopped in and showed her the spot where, he thought, he'd got a piece of glass embedded in his heel.

'I was playing football in Regent's Park,' he explained. 'I'd got my shoes off. It didn't hurt much at first, but it's really throbbing now.'

Abby felt the spot. It was hot and there was a small puncture mark. It was more than likely that he'd got a sliver of something or other in there. She cleaned the area carefully and sprayed it with the pain-killing spray. 'This is probably going to hurt,' she warned him as she began to probe the puncture wound with fine forceps. He winced, but told her to go on.

The glass was deeply embedded and it took her some time, working with tweezers and forceps, to get it out. 'Look,' she offered, after the patient had cried out, 'I'll just bandage you up and we'll take you round to the accident and emergency department at University College Hospital. You'll get a proper local anaesthetic there.'

He looked at her as if she'd made an obscene suggestion. 'I've been to those places before, and all that happens is that you wait for hours, and when you eventually see a doctor they tell you you're making a nuisance of yourself and should have gone to your GP. And they also,' he muttered darkly, 'want to know where you live and what your name is and difficult things like that. You just go on digging it out, Nurse. Give us another squirt of that spray if you want, though. It helps a bit.'

Abby did as she was told, and before long had managed to extricate the glass. Then she swabbed the wound out and bound it with an antibiotic dressing. God only knew what else he'd trodden in while running around barefoot in the park. The last thing he wanted was an infection. Reaching to the bottom of her bag, she took out a sample tube of antibiotic ointment. Knowing the kind of work she was doing, James made a point of passing on to her any potentially useful free samples, and this was one of them. Whenever he gave her anything he told her how mad she was to be doing such a job, and he also made a fuss about not passing her anything that could be potentially dangerous, but secretly she thought he rather enjoyed hearing about what she got up to. Maybe she'd persuade him to come and have a look for himself one day.

'Now, the throbbing should ease, and I've given you a dressing with antibiotic impregnated in it,' she explained, 'but if the pain is still persisting tomorrow I suggest you go to Accident and Emergency, as I told you.' The man started to protest, but she stopped him. 'Now if it's still swollen and painful and you *can't* go, wash your hands, take the dressing off carefully, squeeze some of this on to the wound and put *this* clean dressing over the top. Then come and see me here the next day. And whatever you do, don't take your shoes off again.'

'But I've only got my boots, and they're murder in this heat,' he complained.

'We'll see if Steve can find you a lighter pair. He should have a stock of shoes and clothes here,' Abby suggested.

'Okay, thanks.' He stood up and put some weight on the foot. 'It feels better already. I'll keep it nice and clean for you—the last place I want to end up is hospital!'

Abby washed her hands in the tiny cold-water basin that had been plumbed in. The door of the 'surgery' opened behind her, but she didn't turn round immediately. 'Sit down for a second,' she instructed. She heard the old couch creak as the patient obeyed. With a welcoming smile she turned to find out what the next challenge was to be.

Sam was sitting there, larger than life in the tiny room. He was wearing white cotton trousers and a baggy old chambray shirt, and the finishing continental touch was his blue canvas espadrilles, which he wore without socks. 'It *is* you,' he said wonderingly as she backed away from him.

'James said you'd changed, but he didn't tell me you'd cut your hair off.'

He surveyed her more closely. She'd lost weight; not a lot, but her cheekbones were a shade more prominent, and with her short, stylish crop she looked younger, more vulnerable than she had before. She eyed him warily.

'What are you doing here?'

'I came to see you.' He was several feet away from her, but already she could sense that old magnetic magic beginning to work its charm. She could feel his eyes burning her. 'I came to ask you to forgive me.'

Abby began to pack her equipment methodically into her bag. Used forceps and tweezers went into one box, clean ones into another. The used dressings and cotton wool she placed in a plastic bag to dispose of at home. It was almost as if Sam wasn't there; she couldn't bring herself to speak to him in case he turned out to be some kind of hallucination. In the months since she'd last seen him she'd persuaded herself to look on him as an important but vanished part of her life. Her involvement with him had changed her, and it had been painful. Now she was doing something new and he was in the past.

'How did you know I'd be here?' She kept her tone flat, uninterested.

'James told me. I wrote to Jenny a few weeks ago, just to find out how you all were.'

'She didn't tell me.'

'I asked her not to. But she told me what had been going on—that James was better and that you'd started your training. And so as there didn't seem to be anything to lose, I came back.'

Abby's hands were shaking as she fastened the top of the bag. 'Just to say that you were sorry? Big deal. For my part, I wish you'd stayed wherever you were. And I *don't* want a postcard from you this Christmas.' She finished her task. 'And now I'm going to have a drink with a friend.' She held out her hand to shake his. 'Goodbye, Sam.'

His eyes flashed warningly and then he stretched one long leg across the doorway, barring her exit. 'I suppose I should have expected that. Just listen to me for a minute, will you, Abby? I'm sorry.'

'There's nothing to be sorry about.' She tried to open the door, but he kept his knee firmly against it. 'In fact *I* should be saying thank you. You've been the making of me,

Sam. I've grown up a lot. I've decided what I want to do with myself for the next few years—and having experienced your brand of charm, I'm not likely to be taken in by anyone like you again. Steve!' she yelled, pounding on the door.

'Stop being facetious!' Sam grabbed her wrists and pulled her to him. The firmness of his chest against her, the strength of his arms, both brought back vivid memories of their nights in Venice. She could feel her body automatically responding to him. 'I've flown all the way from Colombo, and I didn't come just to argue with you—'

'In which case you've wasted your time and your air fare,' Abby snapped back. She got no further, because he caught her face in one hand and, turning her mouth to his, kissed her roughly. She twisted out of his grasp and managed to free one of her hands, which she wiped across her mouth.

'What happened?' Sam looked at her disbelievingly. 'You told me you loved me, and I know you weren't lying.'

'And you told me you didn't love me—so what am I supposed to think when you come stalking in here?'

'You've got it wrong. I only told I've

280

never *said* I loved you—'

Abby cast him a withering glance. 'Please, spare me the semantics and let me out. I don't want to see you or speak to you again, do you understand? You've caused me enough distress already.'

'Do you know why I did that? Do you understand why I chose to leave you at the airport when all I really wanted to do was fly back with you?'

Abby tried to pry his foot free of the door, but he just seized her round the waist and pulled her back against him. 'No, I don't know,' she protested, exasperated. 'Mind-reading never was my strong subject. To be honest, I don't really care *why* you did it. You did it and I'm over it. That's all that matters.'

His hands stroked the back of her neck. 'I wish you hadn't had your hair cut. I loved it long.'

'If I'd known you loved me for my hair I'd have sent it to you when I had it chopped off,' Abby said flippantly, trying to ignore the effect of his hands against her hot skin. She felt his lips caressing her first vertebra and her forced anger began to evaporate.

'I love all of you.' He sighed. 'I know it's

difficult to understand, but I only behaved the way I did because I love you. For a long time I wanted to tell you. Then I realised how much it would hurt you when I had to go—and James, too. I thought that if you could just write me off as some uncaring bastard who constantly steals his friend's girl-friends it would be easier. Has James told you that all this has happened before?'

'Yes. I realise it must be a pattern in your life,' Abby said dryly. 'Every seven years or so you'll be coming back, will you, like a bad penny, causing trouble?'

'I'm going to ignore that,' Sam replied. 'I was confused, I admit. I thought you'd fall back in love with James on the rebound, but you didn't. So I'm here for selfish reasons. I don't want you to get involved with another man. I want you to spend the rest of your life with me. Can you even begin to understand what I'm trying to say?'

Abby turned to look at him. His eyes were dark; she sensed a touch of desperation in him. It was very tempting to believe him, to throw herself into his arms and say yes, she'd follow him wherever he went... But she knew him of old. What she was experiencing now was familiar—and it had ended in disaster before. 'Yes, I understand what you're saying—and no, I don't want any part of it,' she told him. 'I'm beginning to cut things out for myself now, and I'm not going to risk getting involved with you again. I'm serious, Sam. You couldn't even begin to appreciate how much you hurt me.'

'If it was that bad, then you'll understand how I felt. There hasn't been an hour, hardly a minute, day or night, when I haven't thought about you, Abby. I dream about you. Every street I walk down I see you there ahead of me. I hear your voice calling me in empty rooms.' He ran his hand across his face. 'A couple of days after I left you in Venice I decided I had to see you again. I couldn't get a flight, so I caught the boat train. I got as far as Charing Cross Station before I realised how stupid I was being, and I sat there, on the platform, for nearly three hours before I could persuade myself to get on a train for Dover and go back.'

'Don't!' Abby could hear her voice beginning to break. 'Don't go on, *please*, Sam. Don't persuade me. I couldn't bear it all over again.'

'I have no intention of ever losing you again.' He felt in his pocket for something. 'I brought this for you.' He held out a ring. It was made of fine filigree gold in an unfamiliar pattern. 'I bought it for you in Sri Lanka. It's a traditional wedding ring. I've got just three days to persuade you to marry me.'

'It's a lost cause.' She forced the words out. 'In a couple of months' time I'll be off on my own adventures. You always said that husband-and-wife teams didn't work out in the kind of conditions you work in, so it's quite out of of the question.' Quite where those cool words were coming from, Abby didn't know. If her heart had been ruling her actions, she would have reached out and taken the ring there and then. But something else seemed to be in control.

'We can make it work. Jenny says you're even more enthusiastic than her about working abroad; that's proved to me that you're not what I thought you were when we first met. You know me better than anyone else. You know that when you marry me you won't be getting a nice home and a car and holidays in the South of France—not for a few years, anyway.'

'That's not what I want!'

'I know. That's why I'm here. I love you and I want you to marry me.' He kissed her again, tenderly this time. 'Don't tell me I've ruined my chances. Tell me you love me still.'

'I'd have to be mad to marry you,' Abby murmured. 'All you've done is hurt me.'

'Don't exaggerate.' He grinned lop-sidedly and she felt her heart lurch. 'I seem to remember that you enjoyed most of Venice. I got very attached to that bed. Say yes, and I promise it can be like that always. Me and you together against the rest of the world. We make a good team, you know that.'

'And what about James?'

'I've spoken to him already. He says that if I can talk you into marrying me then you're welcome to me. He thinks that if I'm married I won't be able to ruin any more of his relationships.'

'You don't take anything seriously, do you?' Abby protested in exasperation.

Sam looked suitably grave. 'All right, then. James cares a lot about you, and he thinks from what you've told him that you'll be happier with me than with him or anyone else. He wants *you* to be happy, and so he's happy for you to marry me.'

Abby mulled it over. 'And what if we can't work together? I don't want to marry you and then have to spend years apart.'

'I've been offered a two-year posting in September. It's in Botswana. They want a doctor and nurse to establish a community health centre. It's an ideal posting for a nurse without much experience. I have to accept and let them know about you by the end of the week.' Sam looked at her with something new in his eyes—something approaching a pleading expression. 'Will you come with me? There's nothing I've ever wanted more.'

'You've really got things tied up perfectly, haven't you?' she said flippantly. 'If I say no I'll really ruin your plans. When are we getting married?'

He grinned. 'I thought about a special licence the day after tomorrow, but that might look a bit hasty. If you'd prefer it, I can come back in August. We could fit in a honeymoon before we set off for Botswana. James has agreed to be best man, whichever date we choose.'

Abby laughed. 'I could do with a month or two to get used to the idea, so maybe August will be best. Where did you put that ring?'

'You'll marry me, then?' He smiled crookedly at her and she could pretend no longer.

'Yes, of course I will. I'll probably regret it...'

'No.' Sam kissed her. 'You'll never regret it, I promise. There's just one thing I want you to promise me in return.'

'And what's that?' Abby asked dubiously.

'You'll grow your hair long again—as long as it was when I first met you.'

'But that'll take years—ten at least!' she laughed.

'I can wait,' was all he said.